RANCHER TAKES HIS LOVE AT FIRST SIGHT

THE RANGERS OF PURPLE HEART RANCH BOOK 5

SHANAE JOHNSON

THOSE JOHNSON GIRLS

Edited by Alyssa Breck

Manufactured in the United States of America
First Edition September 2020

CHAPTER ONE

*J*ordan Spinelli gave the tie around his neck a tug. First right, then left. No matter which way he tugged it, it still felt too tight.

"Feeling like a noose around your neck?" laughed his best friend, David Porco.

"No," denied Spinelli, shifting the cloth while looking at his reflection in the mirror. "The knot is just wrong."

With deft fingers, Spinelli unraveled the knot. The color of the tie was a soft shade of brown with touches of orange that pushed it toward gold, but not quite. Hazel, the shade could be called. But the blending of colors didn't come near the brilliance in her eyes.

"Did you know that the necktie actually originated in Croatia?" Spinelli flipped the collar of his dress shirt up and wrapped the cloth around his neck, making a new knot. "It was a handkerchief made of silk worn by the soldiers around the neck. The soldiers were presented to Louis XIV wearing the style, and he adapted it, calling it *à là croàte*, meaning of the Croats."

"Nope, didn't know that," said Porco. "All I know is that I look good in a tux. Wish I'd gotten married in one instead of jeans and a T-shirt. But I was in a bit of a rush at the time."

Porco had married Jules Capulano within a few hours after meeting her. It wasn't an uncommon feat in this particular corner of America. Quickie marriages were all the rage in this small Montana town that boasted a rehabilitation ranch for Wounded Warriors. Most of the residents of The Purple Heart Ranch had married for convenience. But each marriage had turned into something more, a strong partnership filled with love and devotion.

Spinelli pulled the simple ring from his pocket. Devotion, he could promise his soon to be wife. But love? That wasn't on the table. Romey Capulano didn't believe in romantic love. If anyone had asked

Spinelli a week ago, he would've said he didn't believe in the notion either.

But then he'd seen her, and his mind had... changed.

He looked at himself in the mirror. The tie was straight, a perfectly balanced Windsor knot where each line hit the right angle. His face was clean-shaven, without a hint of stubble. His dark hair was neatly trimmed, resting just above the collar of his tuxedo jacket. His broad shoulders were back and straight, just as he'd been taught in the Army. So why did his knees feel weak?

"Did you know the tuxedo originated in the Hudson Valley of New York around the year 1888?" Spinelli asked the room of men dressed similarly to himself. They each had a tux handy since weddings were as frequent as cattle runs in these parts. "At the time, it only referred to the white jacket that the elite wore when they went out to dinner. The term later came to include the trousers and other accessories associated with the ensemble, and then it was shortened to tux."

Five pairs of eyes stared at him. Keaton lifted his gaze from a list he was making on a small notepad. Grizz scratched at the stubble on his chin. Mac tore his gaze from the window where his wife stood outside, chatting with another woman. Porco and Rusty sighed in unison as they regarded Spinelli.

Spinelli had never been good at reading facial expressions. He could get by on the basics. A smile meant approval. Though sometimes, it could mean mockery. A frown meant disappointment. A scowl meant anger. Currently, all of his friends' stares were blank. He had no idea what that meant?

"I don't recommend you lead with that explanation on your wedding night," said Rusty.

"Romey is a highly intelligent woman," said Spinelli. "She likely already knows that fact herself."

From the first moment he'd laid eyes on her, standing in the pasta section of the grocery store, Romey Capulano's intelligence had been as clear to see as the perfect diamond he clutched in his palm. He'd been admonishing Porco for his hasty marriage based on the notion that Jules had made his heart speed up and put butterflies in his stomach. Spinelli had aptly diagnosed his friend with, not love, but a medical condition. Across the store, he'd sensed someone agreeing with his words. His gaze had been drawn to Romey. When she'd turned to face him, his entire world had tilted with just that one glance.

"Maybe she knows that fact," said Porco, snapping Spinelli back to the present. "But I bet she'll be interested in other things tonight than a history lesson. By the way, Jules and I are going to clear out and let you two have the cottage to yourself for the night."

"Why would you do that?" asked Spinelli.

The others looked at one another. Mac turned entirely from the window, giving Spinelli his full attention. Grizz's lips twitched as though the big man was trying to hold in a giggle. Keaton held his pencil in mid-air, his checklist forgotten.

"I thought you had *the talk* with him," Porco stage-whispered to Rusty, loud enough so that the people out in the halls of the church could've easily heard.

"I did," said Rusty. "But I didn't pull out any diagrams or equations, so I doubt he was listening."

Spinelli vaguely remembered Rusty bringing up Romey and his upcoming wedding earlier in the week while they were at work. Something or other to do with the mating habits of birds and bees. Though why they were talking about pollination and eggs hatching, Spinelli had no idea. He supposed it was a metaphor. But his mind had never been able to wrap around those. He preferred when people simply said what they meant. That's what dictionaries and encyclopedias were designed for.

"Do you mean sex?" All the tightly held expressions relaxed across the features of his friends' faces. Good, he'd gotten that one right. "Our marriage will be purely platonic."

Five pairs of brows rose towards the ceiling. Five jaws went slack enough to reach the floor. Their looks of surprise surprised Spinelli.

"You all know this is a true marriage of convenience. You were all there when we proposed it."

Just a week ago, the Verona Commune where Romey lived and the Vance Ranch where Spinelli lived had been practically at war. With lawyers and regulations rather than guns and ammo. Porco had made a tactical error when he'd accidentally sprayed chemical fertilizer on the organic farm. That move had lost the commune their certified organic status.

To make amends, Porco offered to buy the strip of land he'd contaminated. That piece of land at the edge of the boundary was where Jules and Romey lived. Unfortunately, Porco didn't have enough to cover it. But Spinelli did. The catch was that in order to buy the land, he had to marry someone from there; Romey.

"This is a purely logical relationship," Spinelli went on. "We're coming together to solve a problem."

"Like me and Brenda did when she wanted to sell me a portion of the ranch," said Keaton.

"Exactly," agreed Spinelli.

Now they were getting it. Brenda Vance and Anthony Keaton had also gotten married on the day they'd met so that she could transfer a portion of her land to the training camp Keaton wanted to establish. It had been a practical, business transaction. Though these days, you couldn't pry the two apart with a shovel.

"Then you're going to need to have *the talk*." Keaton put pencil to pad and began scribbling. "With diagrams and equations this time."

Now it was Spinelli who scowled at his friends. Their grins were all definitely mocking this time. He knew they were trying to imply that he wanted more from Romey than what they had both agreed to. But that wasn't true. He always said what he meant and meant what he said.

He wanted to marry this woman to right a wrong that was partially his fault. It had nothing to do with the golden flecks he'd seen in her almond-shaped eyes. Or the way she bit at her lower lip when she was working out a problem. Or the flare of her nostrils when she came up with an answer.

"This is the best thing to happen," said Porco. "I

married the woman who lit a spark in me, and her sister's marrying my best friend."

There Porco went again about that spark. There was no such thing. Spinelli didn't deny that he was attracted to Romey. But it was her mind that he was most interested in. When he'd seen her in the grocery store, he'd been attracted because she had understood what he was saying about love being a medical condition. It was her intelligence, not the fact that her proportions were in the shape of an hourglass.

Thinking about Romey's figure made his heart skip a beat. The knowledge that in just a matter of moments he would take her hand in his and vow to spend the rest of his life with her made his stomach flutter, as though there were butterflies in there. God, he hoped he wasn't coming down with something right before his wedding.

CHAPTER TWO

"*I* don't see why I need to wear a veil." Romey Capulano used the backs of her hands to fluff the thin scrap of lace up and off her face. "It's not like he hasn't seen me before."

The first time she'd seen Jordan Spinelli was etched in her mind indelibly like the carvings on the Rosetta Stone. Problem was, unlike the translation stone which held the key to deciphering Egyptian hieroglyphs, Romey was still having trouble puzzling out her initial reaction to the man who'd come to stand before her in the grocery store a week ago.

The first time Jordan had seen her, he'd stared at her as though she had been the key to deciphering an ancient language. With each step he'd taken toward her, comprehension had appeared to dawn in his dark eyes. She'd felt a pull like there was some invisible force between them, intent on entwining their lives like the double helix of DNA. That, she'd wanted to shout to her lovestruck sister, was the true spark. The spark that created life.

And then the two of them had spent the afternoon debunking the idea of love.

Jordan's points about the symptoms of true love being those of a medical condition had been so astute and perceptive that Romey had sighed. When he'd described the notion of passion as a cocktail of adrenaline, dopamine, and serotonin that mirrored reactions on the battlefield, Romey had become heated by his analogy and had needed to fan herself. When he'd determined that the best way to pick a life partner should be in the same manner that someone searches for a home, her knees felt weak.

Jordan Spinelli was the most rational, the most logical, the most calculating man that she'd ever met. She wasn't going to ruin it all by falling in love with him. It was the stupidest thing she could've ever done.

In the mirror, her cheeks heated and turned the blush ruddy. Romey moved her hands and let the veil fall back into place. Only to have her sister pin it back.

"The veil is tradition," said Jules.

"Says the woman who eloped in a sundress and sandals with a stranger she'd only known for a few hours."

"Yes," Jules sighed, her eyes going dreamy. "David is my true love, you know that."

Romey didn't know that. It was impossible for her to know that. Though she and her twin sister Jules might share the same features, they each had two entirely different ways of seeing the world.

All their lives, Jules had had her head stuck in the clouds. She'd always believed in the mythical, intangible idea of true love.

Romey was the more practical-minded twin. Math made her heart flip. Science was her true passion. But now her heart was racing at the thought of a man. It was entirely unacceptable. But she couldn't seem to get it under control.

Every time she thought about Jordan, her mind would fog, her palms would sweat, her lips would tingle. It was embarrassing. Her, Romey Capulano, was suffering the side effects from those silly women who read romance novels about a white knight on a steed come to rescue them. Or a tall, dark, and handsome stranger come to sweep her off her feet.

Romey's feet were planted firmly on the ground. The problem was Jordan had come in to rescue her. Not for love or anything trifle like that. Jordan had fronted the other half of the money to buy her homestead, the small parcel of land bordering the Vance Ranch and the Verona Commune. The only way the land transfer would work was for Jules and Romey to marry men with money. Their Shakespeare-loving father would've gotten a kick out of that. With the four of them as equal co-owners, they could separate from the commune and it would be granted the organic status it coveted.

It was an elegant solution that she and Jordan had come up with together. Only, now she'd have to see him every day for the rest of her life. Looking in the mirror, Romey saw that her cheeks flushed even redder. But no, that was Patty Hayes brushing blush onto her cheeks.

"Did you know that wearing a veil predates wearing white?" Romey asked. When she got nervous, she always reached for knowledge to shield her. "The ancient Greeks and Romans believed that if a bride wore a veil, it would deter demons from taking over her spirit. They even had bridesmaid's wear veils as well to try and confuse the demons."

"Well, that'll teach bridesmaids or anyone in attendance from trying to upstage the bride," said Patty. She tilted Romey's head to the side and began to work on her other cheek.

"That's the real reason why a father would walk his daughter down the aisle because the veil obstructed her view, and she would bump into things. So, he, or someone, had to walk her down and give her away."

"You don't have to worry about where you're going," said Jules. "I'll be giving you away. And then, tonight after the wedding, David and I are going to make ourselves scarce."

"Why would you do that?" asked Romey.

"So that you and Jordan can... you know... have some time to yourselves."

Time to their selves? They would have a lifetime with each other. Sometimes her sister made no sense.

"Uh oh," said Patty, turning to Jules. "You two have had *the talk,* haven't you?"

The talk? What talk?

"Oh, yes," said Jules. "Laxmi Patel, that's our reproductive health and sexual education teacher on the commune, she was a former tantra instructor. She taught classes on the *Kama Sutra* when we officially entered puberty after our coming of age ceremony."

Oh. *That talk.*

"It's not like that," said Romey. "Remember, this marriage between Jordan and me is practical. We're not in love."

Romey narrowly missed biting her tongue at the statement. She wasn't sure if this was emotional love that she was feeling. It still might be a medical condition. But she was certain it was one-sided. Jordan was far too intellectual to get mixed up in such nonsense.

"Really?" said Patty as she put the final touches on Romey's cheeks. "I've seen the way he looks at you."

"You have?" said Romey. Had her voice gone up an octave with hope?

"That night you invited us over to your land for the communal bonfire, Spinelli couldn't take his eyes off you."

That couldn't be true because whenever she could, Romey had stolen glances at him. He hadn't been looking at her. And when he had looked at her, it was to engage her in conversation about their arrangement. They had spoken practically about their impending nuptials. There hadn't been a single hint of anything more than a business arrangement. Which was what she had always envisioned her marriage to be.

But there had been that moment back at the grocery store. When their gazes had locked for the first time. Had that been a spark in his eyes? Had that been desire curling at his lips? Had his steps brought him to her because he had seen more in her than a like-minded individual? Would he appreciate the fact that they would have the house to themselves tonight, on their wedding night?

Her pulse raced at the thought. Her throat went dry. Her head started to pound erratically until she began to feel faint.

God, she hoped she was coming down with something right before her wedding. A sickness? Maybe madness? Because she wasn't sure she could handle the alternative.

CHAPTER THREE

"Just don't go on about all that science and coding stuff," said Keaton. "Not everyone is as fascinated by numbers as you."

"Brenda loves the algorithm I designed for her to track cattle growth," said Spinelli.

"Yeah," Keaton grinned, getting that far off look that most of Spinelli's married friends were prone to these days. "Well, Brenda's a different kind of woman."

"Whatever you do, just make sure you don't spend all day playing video games anymore," said Grizz.

"Why not? Your wife mopped the floor with my butt in *Call of Duty* last weekend."

A grin tugged at the corner of Grizz's mouth. He got that same faraway look in his eyes as Keaton. "Yeah, but Patty is a different kind of woman."

"Forget these two bozos." Porco took Spinelli by the shoulders and turned him to face him. "If you don't listen to another piece of advice, hear what I'm saying now. Do not ever tell that woman that love isn't real, and all attraction is some chemicals in the brain. No woman wants to hear that."

Around the room, he saw a chorus of bobbing heads nodding in agreement. Spinelli did appreciate the advice his friends were trying to give him about his impending life as a married man. He just deduced that all of them were dead wrong in their guidance.

He and Romey had talked about his work building a virtual reality war game to compliment the training camp's physical fitness courses. He'd gone on and on about coding various aspects of the game, and she'd leaned in, listening with her full attention. She even spoke a few coding languages. True, it was just Python which grade-schoolers could learn. But it went to show that they had yet another thing in common.

When it came to that other thing? Love? Spinelli had never said he didn't believe in love. Just that it was a cocktail of adrenaline, dopamine, and serotonin better suited for the battlefield. That didn't mean it wasn't real. He was certainly feeling a mixture of those charged chemicals coursing through his body as he walked down the aisle of the church.

A rush of adrenaline must've been released because he felt full of energy from his fingertips down to his pinky toes. His heart rate increased, and he felt the blood flowing like a tidal wave through his veins, signaling there was an increase in dopamine in him. Mixed in that cocktail had to be serotonin because his mood was all over the place. He was happy, nervous, anxious all at the same time.

These were the symptoms all of his friends decried was love. If he was experiencing them now, just before his wedding, did that mean that he'd come down with a case of the romance affliction?

He wasn't sure? What he did know was that his soon-to-be wife had spoken aloud her disdain for the notion of love and romance.

There's no such thing as true love.

Those had been Romey's words the first day he'd met her. When he'd been drawn to her. When he hadn't been able to take his eyes off her. When he'd followed her out of the grocery store, unwilling to be parted from her.

He was about to be joined to her in a legal ceremony now. He would have the rest of their lives to figure out what he was feeling. Until then, he'd honor the deal he'd made with her.

"I've got this all under control," Spinelli said. "This will be a practical marriage. You'll see."

None of the men were looking at him any longer. They'd peeled off into the pews to sit with their wives and the families from Romey's commune. The church was decorated with enough flowers to set off the allergies of the whole town. Intermixed with the flowers were gourds, which he'd learned were a symbol of fertility. Streamers mimicking the rainbow hung from the stain glass windows making the religious depictions look as though they were marching in a Pride parade.

All of that escaped Spinelli as the doors at the back of the church opened, and the music began to play.

Spinelli turned, and his heart stopped. That wasn't hyperbole. Or metaphor. Or analogy.

For two full seconds, his heart stopped beating in his chest. His mind blanked. His breath stopped. Was he experiencing an arrhythmia?

He knew he was having a fight or flight response. He wanted to do both. He wanted to fight his way to the woman who'd just entered the doors. He then wanted to fly with her, where no one would question their motives or give advice on how to maneuver the deal they'd struck.

Spinelli had been labeled a genius when he was young. He could do complex math problems in his head. His brain worked in such a way that strings of numbers lined up for him and made sense. With all the codes he cracked, with all the algorithms he'd designed, this was his most brilliant scheme. Getting Romey Capulano to agree to marry him.

"Breathe," Porco whispered in his ear.

Spinelli did. He inhaled as Romey walked slowly toward him. Her veil fluttered around her face. The thin slip of fabric she wore hid nothing. His heart thumped harder, louder, as though it was trying to escape its cage, the closer she got. At least it had started beating again.

It took everything in him to stand still and wait for her. Though he was standing, he felt like his world was upside down. Not head over heels because that was impossible. Just off-center, because his entire axis had shifted and everything was focused on her.

"Who gives away this woman?" asked Pastor Vance.

"I do," said Jules.

Spinelli had hardly spared Jules a glance even though she was the spitting image of Romey. The two didn't compare in his mind. Jules was sunshine on a warm day. Romey was a supernova.

When the veil lifted to reveal her face, Spinelli's breath caught again. His heart threatened to stop and stare. He'd never seen Romey with makeup. He didn't prefer it, but he couldn't deny its appeal.

Her eyes twinkled. Her golden-brown cheeks were warmed. And her lips...

It took everything in him to hold himself back from claiming those lips right now in front of the whole town. Luckily, he knew there was a part in the ceremony that would allow for him to press his mouth to hers. It was the part after the minister declared Romey his before God and all assembled. Spinelli wanted to skip straight to that part.

His gaze caught on something sparkling from her ear. From her ear hung a silver spiral. It was the pattern of a coral shell. But all Spinelli could think was that it looked like a tornado. Possibly because he felt like the delicate spirals hanging from her earlobes could easily knock him over.

"What is it?" Romey asked.

"It just looks like you're wearing the Fibonacci sequence in your ears," he said.

"It is a visual representation of the Fibonacci sequence." She touched a finger to the dangling spirals. "I use it in my work."

"You never told me that." Spinelli stepped closer, wanting to learn more about her work, wanting to learn more about her. "Did you know that Fibonacci's Golden Ratio is used in computer coding and game design?"

A throat cleared behind them. They both swiveled their heads to see Pastor Vance standing between them. The pastor didn't look annoyed as he regarded them, he looked amused.

"Do you mind getting to know each other better later?" asked Pastor Vance. "We have a pressing engagement happening right now."

"Oh, sorry," Romey said, looking out at the crowd of those gathered. Every face in the pews was as amused as the pastor at their little interlude.

Spinelli wasn't sorry. His head was clear. His heartbeat steady. His nerves were calm.

Porco might go on about The One in an ethereal sense. Spinelli knew that Romey was the one for him in every logical sense.

CHAPTER FOUR

*C*ool logic was all Romey needed to get through this. It didn't matter that her makeup was better than she ever could've done herself. It didn't matter that her wild locks were tamed into a sleek bun, sitting obediently at the back of her head. It didn't matter that the white dress fit her like a glove highlighting all of her best assets and making it appear that she had more than she truly did.

This Romey was an optical illusion, a trick of contouring and highlights. She and Jordan knew the truth. They knew what they were doing here.

So why did her heart skip a beat when the Wedding March started? Why did her fingertips alternate between tingling and numbness as she took her first step down the aisle? Why did she have trouble taking in a full breath when she gazed all the way down toward the end of the aisle and saw him?

Romey's brain scrambled for an explanation. She knew that heart palpations were caused by overheating, or stress, or sugar, or hormones. It had to be one of those factors.

Taking a step down the aisle, she reasoned that she wasn't hot in the dress. The air vents of the church were cool on her back. So, overheating was crossed out.

Her next step was steady, without a wobble in sight. That was because she knew exactly what she was doing. She and Jordan had made a very thorough plan for this union. There were no unknowns. Which meant she wasn't stressed out.

It wasn't her time of the month. She'd made sure when she'd made the plan for the wedding day. They'd planned for a weekday wedding, on a Tuesday afternoon. Their families and friends had balked at the idea. Weddings should be on the weekends, they'd insisted. But neither Romey nor Jordan saw a reason why? For them, this was business as usual. So why not have it on a business day.

Her sister was still emotional about that

decision. Romey had merely shrugged then. She internally shrugged now. Proving that she wasn't having a hormonal episode.

That left sugar. Patty had brought her a glass of sweet tea before she'd begun painting her face. Romey had only taken one sip before getting a head rush at the glass of sugar that was accompanied by a splash of water and a few tea leaves. Growing up on a vegan commune, table sugar wasn't a hot commodity. Those crystals were clearly having a wayward effect on her as she made her way towards her husband to be.

She felt the overwhelming need to fan herself as her soon to be husband came into view. Jordan was dashing in his tux. Romey's mouth went dry, and she wished she could take another sip of that sugary tea.

Her cheeks were heating. She was short of breath. Her makeup was likely melting away from the sweat collecting at her brow. Thank goodness for the veil. She didn't want Jordan to see her like this. But seeing him standing there, waiting for her, did something to her mind. The many brain cells she possessed all scrambled to fall in line with the erratic beating of her heart.

This could not be happening to her. Romey was

not falling in love. She was too smart for that. She didn't believe in that.

She needed to get a grip. This wasn't part of the plan. Only... why was Jordan looking at her with his mouth agape? Why was he scratching at his chest? Was he having heart palpitations as well? Maybe they were both sick? Maybe something was going around?

She wished with all her heart that they were coming down with the flu and not... the other thing. A glance to her right and left showed that no other person in the church was experiencing the same symptoms.

As she took her last step, Jordan reached for her. Without hesitation, Romey took his hand. The moment their fingers made contact, something zinged across her fingertips. It bounced off the center of her palm. It zipped up her arms and spread warmth through her chest.

She had to face facts. She wasn't sick. She had simply lost her mind. And she was so screwed.

"Dearly beloved," began Pastor Vance. "We are gathered here today to witness the union of Romey Supernova Capulano and Jordan Jefferson Spinelli."

Jordan raised his brow at the mention of her middle name. Romey waved it away. Her parents had been hippies and allowed her to choose her own middle name. She had been into astronomy at the time.

"We will begin with the vows—"

"Actually, Pastor Vance," Romey interrupted. "Jordan and I have written our own vows."

Pastor Vance chuckled under his breath. He closed his Bible and then made a magnanimous motion with his hand. The bride and groom turned to face their guests.

In the pews was a colorful collective of people. It was very clear to see who belonged to whom. The soldiers and families from the Vance and Purple Heart ranches were all decked out in collared shirts, flannel, and sundresses. Meanwhile, on Romey's side of the aisle, kente cloth mixed with feathered headdresses, and vibrant saris.

The best part was that no one was fighting. Their two worlds were coming together. True, there was still clearly a line of division that was the aisle separating the two sides. But this was a great start.

"As you know," Romey said, "we are both scientists."

"As such, it's research that informs our decisions and our actions," said Jordan.

"So, we decided that there would be no better

way to pledge our lives to each other than with scientific research and data."

The crowd of married couples, domestic partners, and friends turned to one another. A few from either side even looked over the dividing line for a clue of what was happening.

"We have crafted our vows as specific objectives based on data." Romey turned to Jordan before continuing. "Jordan, from this moment forth, I vow to respect you for who you are, and show appreciation for who you endeavor to become."

"Thank you, Romey." Jordan nodded to her and then addressed the crowd. "This vow is based on the Theory of Positive Illusions, which shows that it is advantageous to see a life partner in the most positive light instead of highlighting their flaws."

"Exactly," Romey agreed, standing side by side as they addressed their families and friends.

Behind them, Romey thought she heard Pastor Vance utter an *oh, Lord*.

"To further illustrate the efficacy of this vow," Romey continued, "we turn to Michelangelo's Phenomenon, which shows the value in supporting each other's attempts to better ourselves over time as beneficial for the mutual partnership."

"Pretty hard to refute a great such as

Michelangelo." Jordan nodded. "Romey, as our lives intertwine, I vow that your choices will always be yours and yours alone. Which means that I will never obstruct your freedom."

There was a snort from the peanut gallery. Romey narrowed her eyes, seeking out the culprit. It looked like a number of individuals on both sides were doing a poor job of keeping a straight face. Well, they could laugh it up. Just give it a couple of years, and they'd see whose marriages were still happy and whole based on a racing heart. Emotions were fleeting. Science was forever.

Whatever was going on with her internally would pass. These vows would ensure they would maintain a mutually beneficial union until their dying days. With that thought, Romey continued.

"Thank you, Jordan. For those of you that don't know that vow of non-obstruction comes from remarkable research based on the Social Construct of Autonomy, which postulates that humans, as social creatures, need and enjoy relationships but also must maintain individuality. Therefore, there will be no pressuring or guilting or coercing on either of our parts."

Another round of snickers and giggles riffled through the audience. Romey didn't bother to ferret out the guilty parties. She turned from the crowd to face the man that mattered.

Her heart had settled down now. She was breathing normally. Her head was clear. Whatever she'd been feeling earlier had been a passing phase.

"Romey, I vow to treat you with compassion rather than fairness. I vow this because we are a team where one whole and one whole make two and not one."

Just like that, her heart began skipping beats again. Romey had seen these words written down on paper. She'd sat beside Jordan as they'd constructed the pledges. But, for some reason, hearing them spoken out loud, in his deep baritone, changed the meaning of the words.

"This vow is based on Communal Orientation," Jordan continued. "It assures that we won't keep track or tabs. We will both contribute to the relationship based on our strengths and not on a tally system."

Romey expected more heckling laughter. All was silent. Except for her beating heart. The sound of it filled her ears. The only thing holding her up was Jordan's hand, which she belatedly realized, still held hers.

His thumb rubbed lightly across her knuckles.

Her fingertips rested in the cradle of his palm. She had the urge to step closer to rest her head on his chest. But that wasn't part of the plan.

"Is that all of the vows?" Pastor Vance stepped forward. "That was very... academic. Do you have the rings?"

Both David and Jules stepped forward with the rings. They both were simple affairs. Just gold bands. Romey had declined the addition of a diamond with all the work she did in the dirt. But something sparkled at her from the band, a tiny, perfectly cut diamond.

"Now, according to God's holy ordinance, I pronounce you man and wife. You may kiss the bride."

Romey and Jordan had discussed each vow. They had footnoted and referenced each theory upon which their lives together would be based. They had not once discussed the kissing aspect of the ceremony.

Jordan still held onto her hand. With his free hand, he lifted his fingers to her chin and tilted her face up. Romey looked up in time to see Jordan's face coming towards her. When his lips met hers, she lost her breath.

He brushed once. Twice. On the third touch, he held, letting his lips linger.

Tiny, illogical sparks of emotion glittered over every part of her skin. Her heart didn't race anymore. It settled down, as though it had found a new home. Despite all evidence to the contrary, it appeared that Romey was wrong. That thing called romantic love might have some validity after all.

CHAPTER FIVE

*T*here was a phenomenon called phantom limb. It was where an amputee felt as though their lost limb was still attached. An itch in a foot that was no longer there. An ache in a wrist where the forearm was gone. Long moments after he'd broken the kiss that pronounced them man and wife, Spinelli could still feel the warm pressure of Romey's mouth upon his lips.

The kiss had been fleeting, but in the all too short space in time that he'd been joined with her at the mouth, he had memorized the curve of her top lip. He knew the precise angle of the divot that marked the right half of her upper lip to the left. He knew the exact internal temperature of her body from the heat given off the slight exhalation when she'd gasped. He knew she'd had strawberries for breakfast.

The kiss had been an hour ago, but Spinelli was still feeling its effects. Still wrapped up in all of the sensory detail. Like it was a phantom limb.

Which was illogical. Romey was not a part of his body.

So why did he feel her absence so acutely even when she sat right next to him at the reception table?

Why, no matter how many times he licked his lips, or pressed them together, could he not shake the ghostly sensation?

"Here's to my best friend, Jordan Spinelli."

Spinelli broke out of his reverie. The sun had set over the Vance Ranch. Picnic tables were arrayed out back of the big house. For the first time ever, the neighbors from the Verona Commune walked freely across the pastures. There hadn't been a single argument between the ranchers and the farmers the entire wedding day.

Porco stood front and center, glass raised to deliver the Best Man speech. The phrase was ironic. In days of old, the Best Man was actually the best swordsman a groom could find. Because a sword might be needed to defend the groom against the bride's family. Bridal kidnapping was a lucrative enterprise throughout history.

In a way, Spinelli had stolen his bride. They could've found loopholes in the commune's charter. With both his and Romey's brain together, no unsolved equation or legalese would've stood in their way.

"Spinelli has always kept us in line with his calculations," said Porco. "His current math has brought him the best problem."

Spinelli hadn't bothered with the math. He hadn't given the charter a single glance. He'd arrived at this solution in the blink of an eye, with flimsy logic, and held to it. He'd stolen his wife, and he had not a single regret.

"His mathematical mind has brought him a woman who will keep him on his toes because her mind matches his own."

Spinelli looked over at his wife. Romey brushed her lip with her fingers, a slight blush touched her caramel-colored cheeks. Spinelli had the insane urge to brush a kiss against those lightly freckled cheeks to determine if they would be sweet and warm like the sugary confection.

"These two think they're solving a problem. But I

hope the solution will lead them to see that they are a perfect fit."

Romey turned, as though sensing Spinelli's eyes on her. Her gaze widened when she saw that they were. Her hand jerked away from her mouth and slipped beneath the table.

The strangest thought arose in his mind. He saw himself drawing a sword against anyone who would try to take her from him. Clearly, he'd had too much to drink. Though his wine glass was untouched.

"Jordan, you've tried to talk sense into me more times than I can count," Porco went on. "I rarely listened, but you were always there to pick up the pieces and say I told you so, with a historical or mathematical anecdote that I never understood."

The crowd laughed. Spinelli didn't get the joke. He had done all those things. Porco's statement was factual, not funny.

"You told me Jules and I were incompatible. You were wrong. But you stood by me and tried to help me win her. When you and Romey came up with this idea to marry so that we could all buy the land and save the commune, I thought it was crazy. But then I thought about it and realized you two are perfect for each other."

Beside Spinelli, Romey shifted in her chair. She

placed her hands back on the covered table and rubbed at the ring he'd put on her finger. The ring had belonged to his Sicilian grandmother. Sicilians believed diamonds were forged by the fires of love. Egyptians believed the wedding band circle meant that the couple was entering into a never-ending cycle.

Spinelli didn't buy into any of that mythological nonsense. There was reasoning in the ring and its placement. Wedding bands and engagement rings were placed on the left hand's fourth finger because there was a vein leading to the heart, the *vena amoris*. Meaning he'd laid a direct path to Romey's heart. He liked the sound of that science.

"You both are smart, loyal, and no one understands you," Porco was saying. "Except for the two of you. You get each other."

Spinelli knew his friend was going for more laughs at their expense. And Porco was getting them. What his best man didn't realize was that the statement was true.

Over the last week, Spinelli had watched as Romey spoke to others. They often nodded at her with confused expressions. Meanwhile, her every word made complete and total sense to Spinelli.

"Jordan Spinelli, you have been my brother in

arms, but now you are my brother-in-law. Romey got a good deal, but I'm the luckiest man in the world."

There were a few jeers from the soldiers in the room. Many cheers from the women. And a cacophony of whoops, jingling bells, stomping, and high pitched yelps from the colorful people of the commune. Everyone raised their glasses and toasted to Romey and Spinelli's happiness.

Two cakes were brought out after the toast. One was vegan, the other was not. Spinelli brought the vegan cake forward on the table to cut. He had no intention of giving up meat or dairy, but he wanted his wife to be comfortable. It was in their peer-reviewed, fact-checked vows.

"This will be our first joint task in married life," Romey said as she came to stand next to him before the crowd.

Spinelli placed his hand over hers on the knife. A zing went up his palm. He flexed his fingers, pumping them into a fist to shake off the sensation. He needed to get control over himself.

Apparently, Romey was having the same problem with controlling her appendages. Her fingers trembled on the knife's handle. Jordan put his hand back over hers. Her trembling ceased immediately. A calm washed over him at the rightness of her hand in his.

They sliced through the cake, making perfect, evenly spaced triangles. The geometry of it sent his heart racing. They sliced all the way around until they came to the last piece; three hundred and sixty degrees of perfection.

Romey tilted her head back and looked up at him. Her smile was a triumph at their accomplishment. His gaze dipped to her lips. Everything in him told him to lean down and capture her plump top lip. To tease her lower lip. To press her to him until he didn't know where he ended and she began.

Was he truly losing it? Or did the little twinkle in her hazel eyes tell him she wanted the same? Eyes were the window to the soul had always been a metaphor he didn't understand. If one could look into the eyes, they'd see into the brain. Was Romey's brain giving him permission to claim her lips?

It was the catcalls that brought them back to the task at hand. With a heavy heart, Spinelli let go of his wife's hand. With her warmth no longer in the palm of his hands, his fingers shook again. His mouth ached to recapture the pressure from earlier.

Because his lips were denied, they tingled even more.

He took a few deep breaths. When that didn't work, he stuffed a slice of the vegan cake in his mouth. Only to come away surprised at the velvety texture of the concoction. He must truly be losing his mind if he found himself enjoying the flour-less, butter-less, dairy-free dessert.

Spinelli had promised Romey a logical marriage. But here he was thinking of ravaging her out under the stars like some love-sick fool. Because, maybe, he was a lovesick fool. Which was the worst thing that could possibly happen to him in this relationship.

He needed to hide his feelings from her. He needed to regain his rational mind. He knew that's what she liked, and Spinelli wanted Romey to like him. He wanted to please her. He wanted to make her heart speed up and her breath catch. He wanted her to want him the way he wanted her. But if he told her that, if he showed that, it would ruin everything.

Spinelli turned away from his wife. His gaze fastened on the top of the cake. There was a decoration there; a tanned groom and a brown-skinned bride topped the cake. Aside from the skin color, there was no likeness to the two of them.

"The top of the cake is traditionally saved to be used at the first child's christening," he said.

"Yes, I know," Romey said. "It's supposed to be good luck if a birth happens in a year."

"Well, we won't need to save ours."

He took the decoration off the top of the cake and placed it in the trash with the other discarded plates. That should let her know he was committed to the logical arrangements within their marriage. Except when he looked at her, she wasn't smiling at him as though they were of two minds. She was staring at the trash can and frowning.

CHAPTER SIX

*R*omey stared at the plastic couple in the trash heap. They didn't resemble her and Spinelli, not really. The artist hadn't captured Spinelli's strong jaw and massive shoulders that were like a great brown bear's. Neither did the bride figurine look much like Romey. The plastic caricature's hair was smooth, nothing like Romey's springy hair that would never be permanently tamed. And there were no freckles on the molded woman's cheeks.

She couldn't truly blame the artist. Romey's features didn't fit any mold. Most people drew redheads with freckles. Romey's mother had been a redhead. The freckles on Romey's cheeks were brown and not red. Her hair was a mixture of brown and black with touches of gold.

Her father had said his daughters' hair was like flames. Jules had smiled at that, taking the words as a compliment. Romey had frowned at the statement, taking it as fact. Fire didn't have brown in its spectrum.

Romey had had to work all her life to understand when someone was making light and when someone was stating factual information. She wished people only stated facts and conclusions. She had such difficulty with anything else.

Which was why she liked Jordan so much. He only spoke in factual statements. So when he'd tossed the figurine couple into the trash, Romey knew he had no plans to procreate with her.

Had she wanted progeny? She didn't know? She'd never truly thought about it. She'd never truly thought she'd get married. No one had ever shown that kind of interest in her. The few times she thought a boy might have been interested in her looks, he quickly changed his mind after she opened her mouth and gave a glimpse of the contents of her brain.

Romey questioned everything. She thought

deeply about everything. She was the girl who, when watching a movie, wanted to talk about and dissect not only the plot but the technical aspects of the films.

For example, whenever the hunky heartthrob was at a school dance, or the action hero stumbled into a night club, it made no sense to Romey that they could have a private conversation with the love interest amid the band or blaring speakers. While the audience was held rapt with attention at the whispered words, Romey's mind couldn't suspend her disbelief. So, of course, she'd gone and researched the technique.

In the film world, the sound technique was known as the phenomenon of Figure Ground. It was a rule in filmmaking that allowed for the singling out of an event that is made to be important and making it the only thing the audience could hear. But just because they made it a rule in celluloid didn't mean it made sense in reality.

The music from two loudspeakers filled the night's air. The tune was an upbeat favorite. The makeshift dance floor filled with cowboys, soldiers, and second-generation flower children.

"Are you all right?"

Jordan's words were spoken quietly beside her ear. Through the cacophony of the music and shouts of the people at the reception, she heard him perfectly. Everything had quieted around her until only his voice, his words were in focus.

He stood as close to her as was possible without touching. But the heat coming off of him made her shiver. Which was entirely nonsensical. How was it that the opposite of normal kept happening when she was with him? For a man that appreciated her intelligence, she found herself tongue-tied at times when speaking to him.

Jordan was so handsome. Smart men shouldn't have that amount of beauty. It was becoming harder and harder for her to concentrate when she looked at him. Her mind kept focusing on the perfect asymmetry of his eyes. The angles of his jaw. The arcs and curves of his lips.

"I'm fine," Romey said.

Jordan opened his mouth. His lips quivered as if he was having the same kind of trouble forming words as she was. Could he be feeling the same effects as her? There was a bit of sweat on his brow. His nostrils were flaring. Did his gaze just dip to her lips?

"Time to toss the bouquet." The shout came from Jules, who was standing just a few feet from them.

Jordan fairly leaped away from Romey. His hand went to his brow. He used the back of his hand to wipe away the sweat. Then he scrubbed his palm over his nose and mouth. When his face emerged, he wore the calm and self-possessed demeanor which had first attracted Romey to him.

She'd been wrong. There was no passion for her there.

Romey allowed herself to be pulled away from her husband. She needed the breathing room from the man. There were times when he made her feel so focused, like when they were researching academic archives for their vows. Then there were times when her mind fogged, like when he flashed her a grin over a discussion of the latest scientific find of an exoplanet that contained water vapor.

Just the thought of him grinning at set Romey's pulse racing, her heart beating, and her mind whirring in a mist of fog.

"Uh oh," said Jules with a grin.

"What?" Romey looked down at her dress, but she hadn't spilled anything on it yet. Which was a miracle. She could never get through a day without dirt finding its way onto her clothing.

"I think you like him." Jules' voice carried over the lyrics easily. Unfortunately.

"Of course I like him," Romey hissed. "I married him."

"No, I think you *like him*, like him."

Romey had always hated those kinds of statements. It was grammatically incorrect to use a verb as its own adverb. And *like* wasn't even a verb.

"I'm not that girl," Romey said. She wasn't now and had never been. Her teenage bedroom had been plastered with the Periodic Table and equations not obnoxious boy band posters.

"No?" asked Jules, sounding genuinely curious. "What if Jordan is that guy?"

But Jordan wasn't that guy. He was a mathematical genius, a brilliant computer coder. Which meant that he was a numbers guy, and not so good with words. Which was what Romey had reasoned that she'd wanted in a life partner. Right?

David came up behind Jules. He slipped his arms around his wife and pressed a kiss to her head. The move was thoughtless but held so much tenderness. Romey had never experienced that kind of care or tenderness from any man except her father. She doubted Jordan would ever make such a move on her. It wasn't outlined in their vows.

Despite herself, Romey had come to like her new brother-in-law. She liked all the men and women on the Vance Ranch. Even Brenda Vance Keaton was growing on her. The female rancher had asked Romey and Jules tons of questions about their soybean crop as she fed it to her cattle, who grazed voraciously on the lands. Brenda was a smart woman, which Romey admired. Not at all cutthroat as those on the Verona Commune had been led to believe.

Romey spied Brenda and her husband Keaton, stealing a kiss as they swayed slowly to the upbeat music. Much of those gathered were couples in loose embraces, or touching, or looking at one another with the same light of tenderness that David looked at Jules. The same love that her father had gazed upon her mother with.

When she found Jordan's gaze, it wasn't trained on her. He was looking off into the distance. His expression was unreadable, as always.

Romey felt another thud in her heart. But this time, it wasn't a pleasurable skipping of a beat. This time it hurt, like tripping over her feet and falling down with a resulting bruise. Had she just made the biggest mistake of her life?

It was too late now. It was done. The music

quieted, and all eyes were on her at the center of the dance floor. She was sure whatever woman who would caught the bouquet would find it a blessing. Because that woman would be smarter than Romey. The odds were that that woman would marry a man whom she loved, and who loved her back.

CHAPTER SEVEN

The disease was spreading. Now not only did Spinelli feel a phantom pang on his lips, but it had also moved to his hands. He was repeatedly clenching and unclenching his fists. He rubbed his fingers against his pant legs, seeking the friction there to erase what he'd touched. Nothing helped. No matter what he did, he couldn't get the thought out of his mind that he needed to touch Romey again. To hold her to him. To place his lips upon hers.

He'd almost taken her into his arms before Jules had come up. If Jules hadn't interrupted, what would he have done? He knew exactly what he'd have done. He would've kissed his wife right there, under the stars, in front of everyone they knew, and for no logical reason. Other than he couldn't stop himself.

He had to get himself in order. The two of them had worked so hard on their vows, worked so hard to make this a marriage of mutuality and logic. Now he was going to blow it. All because of that ceremonial kiss.

Spinelli had kissed girls before. Those times had just been the press of skin against skin. All the while, his mind had been elsewhere. Thinking over his latest computer codes and algorithms. Which was probably a factor in the reasoning of why he rarely got a second date with girls.

A wandering mind hadn't been the case when he'd kissed Romey. Spinelli had spent so much time talking to her, getting to know her mind, and her thoughts. So much so that when he kissed her, his mind had been focused solely on her. And now he wanted more. More of her words and definitely more of her kisses.

"It's time for our newlywed's first dance as a married couple."

Across the crowded area, Spinelli's gaze found Romey's. Then they were moving towards each other. He was the moon being pulled into her earthly orbit. There was nothing he could do to resist the gravity of her.

A slow song played over the loudspeakers. The song was sappy and stringy. Spinelli found himself pulling Romey into his arms.

She came to him without protest. Though her brows were knitted in concern. She'd seen through him. She'd seen that the madness of illogic was infecting his entire being. Would she ask for an annulment? Based on reasons of insanity. Because that's what he was experiencing.

She didn't pull away. She pressed her body against his, fitting perfectly into his arms. Just like he'd heard so many romantics say; she fit perfectly.

His large hand spanned the small of her back. She came up to the perfect height if he wanted to lean down and kiss her. Which he wouldn't do. But oh, how he wanted to.

His arms tightened around her. She didn't protest. Her knitted brows relaxed. There was trust in her eyes. More than anything, Spinelli wanted to keep that trust. He wanted Romey to know that she could depend on him. This was just a momentary lapse in his normally clear-minded brain.

Even as he thought it, he heard the lie reverberating in his mind.

"Do you want children?"

At the sound of Romey's words, the hand Spinelli had at her back shook. His fingers curled into the fabric of her dress. It took two deep breaths to get himself under control and release his clenched fingers.

"I'm sorry," she said, shaking her head and looking away. "We didn't discuss that in our negotiations. It was an oversight."

"Do you want children?" He was surprised his voice didn't come across as shaky because inside him, everything was rocking.

Romey bit her lip, lost in thought.

Spinelli held his breath as he watched. He would give anything to be that tooth. The thought of the process of making children with this woman overwhelmed him. At the very least, he'd get to kiss her again. Though the act of kissing wasn't at all necessary to create offspring. Which seemed such a waste.

"I do," she said finally.

"You do?" And then he realized. "Me, too."

Beyond the thought of sharing Romey's kiss and her body, he wanted to see a springy haired kid running around in the fields. He wanted to teach his son or daughter to make planes and build circuits and code games.

"Someday."

Spinelli jerked back to the present. It took him a moment to realize Romey had introduced a qualifier. *Someday*. He needed her to be precise with her language. Exactly how long would he have to wait?

He also wanted to clarify how they would go about it. She could've meant adoption or in vitro fertilization. He did not want a sterile environment when it came to the creation of their children.

"We have our trial period to go through first, of course," she said.

"Trial period?" Again he clutched her closer. Just the thought of this ending was too much for him.

Romey gasped. It was only a slight sound, and she quickly composed herself. But her breath touched his lips, making him hungrier.

"Of course," she said. "This is only the first round of our marriage project. There are bound to be a few kinks along the way that we'll need to work out. Best have that sorted before we add new variables, like children, to the project."

She was right. But he didn't relax his hold on her. She didn't try to pull away.

He couldn't take his eyes off her. There was so much symmetry in her face. The left and right sides of her face weren't complete mirror images of one another, which was impossible in the natural world. But it was darn sure close.

Spinelli had studied the scientific definition of beauty. Romey met all the qualifications. The distance between her eyes was just under half the width of her face. The space between her eyes and mouth was just over one-third the height of her face. She was practically perfect.

That had to be the reason he found himself so attracted to her. She was textbook beautiful.

"You're beautiful."

He hadn't meant to say the words. But they were on his mind. He'd never learned the trick of keeping his thoughts to himself.

"It's the makeup and the gown," she said, still not meeting his gaze. "They highlight my best assets."

Her smile was hesitant. Had he made her uncomfortable? He'd need to keep these overtures to a minimum, preferably none at all. Clearly, Romey wasn't interested in her physical features. Trial project or not, that's not what this marriage would be about.

"Our children will be beautiful with big brains,"

Spinelli said, trying to cover his attraction and remind her that he was a genius, which was one of the qualities she admired most about him.

"Brains, beauty, and brawn," Romey agreed.

Her hand came to rest on his bicep. He could feel the heat of her palm through two layers of fabric. His muscles flexed under her fingers, eager to show off for her. He wanted Romey to know that he would provide for her, he would protect her, and someday, he would procreate with her.

Her gaze found his then. Spinelli couldn't hide what was in his mind, what was in his heart. He wanted his wife, to kiss her, to hold her, to whisper in her ear.

Whisper what? He wasn't sure. Maybe he could rattle off the golden ratio of the Fibonacci sequence. Surely she would like that since she wore the symbolic spiral of the sequence in her ears.

Before he could open his mouth, whether to rattle off the sequence of numbers or kiss her parted lips, they were pulled apart. The cheering and catcalling turned their attention back to their friends and family. Every pair of eyes were on them, whooping, whistling, making kissing noises.

"Logical relationship?" shouted Porco. "Yeah, right."

Romey stiffened in Spinelli's arms. She pressed her once parted lips together. Then she turned to him, the cool consideration that had first attracted him firmly in place.

"I think we've provided enough entertainment for them," she said. "You ready to call it a night?"

That was met with more revelry from the group and a few lewd gestures from his friends. Spinelli knew from past experience that trying to explain anything away to this group would amount to nothing. So, he draped an arm over Romey's shoulders and turned them to go.

Rice flew at their backs. Another strange tradition of the wedding ceremony. The throwing of rice was meant to symbolize rain. Which, in turn, symbolized fertility.

There would be no need for fertility tonight. But, Spinelli reminded himself, there might be someday. If he could hold true to the vows he'd made to his wife. Vows that didn't include the thoughtless passion which they were now being heckled about.

It was going to be a hardship, keeping his hands and his feelings from this woman. But he knew that if he wanted to keep her, if he wanted to get to someday, he would have to try harder to master the irrationality that had taken hold of him today.

Because Romey was the perfect woman for him -for his mind, his body, and, yes, even his heart. And he would do any and everything to keep her. Even if that meant denying himself the pleasure of her kisses.

CHAPTER EIGHT

*I*n the early morning light, Romey gathered a handful of her curls. Her fingers tugged at them from the roots, separating her hair into sections. She used a fat-tooth comb and started plucking at the unruly ends, which much preferred to stick together than hang on their own. When she was younger, she'd let her hair lock into permanent plaits, like her sister. But Romey had grown frustrated with the long locks constantly getting in her way as she happily dug in the dirt each day. So she'd shorn them off with gardening shears.

Her father, who placed inner beauty over physical beauty, had shrugged. Her mother, ever non-conforming to the feminine ideal, had beamed at her daughter's uneven and lopsided new do. Jules, who'd at the time liked having a live mirror to gaze into, was distraught, thinking she'd have to do the same. Romey had only cared that her hair was out of her way so that when she leaned over her notebooks to record her data, her hair wasn't getting in the way.

From that day forward, she'd routinely shorn off her locks, ensuring they never grew beyond the nape of her neck. As she combed out the first tuft, she let the lock of hair fall down and saw that it was nearly touching her shoulders. Looking into her vanity, the evidence was clear. It was time for a cut.

So why was she hesitating to reach for the scissors?

On her wedding day, Jordan had said she looked beautiful. Sure, she was wearing a dress that highlighted all that was good on her figure. But it was a dress she never planned to wear again. And her face had been painted to accent certain parts of her features. A long process which she had no time nor inclination to repeat each morning. But she hadn't done much with her hair. Had that beauty he'd noted encompassed her hair?

Romey turned from the scissors, deciding she could go a few more days before a hair cut. Out of the corner of her eye, she spied a makeup kit. She reached for the kit, turning it over in her hands like a penny flipped through the knuckles. It wouldn't hurt to shade the bags under her eyes from her poor sleep last night.

That wasn't vanity. It was practical. She didn't want anyone asking questions or making innuendo about her late-night activities. Because there had been none.

Jordan had retired to her parents' old room, now his room. She had walked into her bedroom. Alone. As was planned.

Jules and David had spent the night out. They hadn't come home last night, and Romey hadn't heard a peep to indicate they'd returned this morning. It was just her and Jordan and the bags under her eyes.

Were the dark circles getting bigger? Would he notice? Would he still think her beautiful this morning in a T-shirt, shorts, and no makeup?

She looked down at the case of eye shadow. Before she could make up her mind whether or not to open it, she spied the expiration date. It was two years expired.

She could go into Jules' room and grab her kit. Whenever they needed to get dressed up, it was always Jules who did Romey's hair and makeup.

Romey tossed the entire kit into the trash. What

was she thinking? Primping for her husband? David had agreed to marry her for reasons that had nothing to do with her looks.

The sound of padding footsteps came from the hall. It was followed by a door opening and close. Then the sound of the shower starting.

Romey swallowed. Her husband was in the bathroom, just next door, stepping into a shower without a stitch on. She'd felt Jordan's muscles. What would they look like glistening with soap and suds?

Romey gave herself a shake. She should not be having thoughts like that. She would not. He was her husband, not her lover.

Love and romance were not a part of the equation that they'd calculated together. She had no idea why those variables kept trying to insinuate themselves into this carefully constructed mathematical statement. Because it was null.

Jordan didn't see her that way. He saw her as a smart, competent woman. That's who she was.

Romey scrubbed a hand over her bare face. She shoved a headband over her hair and stood. He said he took her as she was. Well, this was her. Dingy shorts with permanent grass stains. A worn T-shirt of a cat holding a bone with the caption *I found this humerus*. No makeup. No muss. No fuss.

She walked to her bedroom door. When she opened it, she heard the shower stop. She froze, wondering if he'd come out fully dressed. Or if he'd come out in a towel. She was far too chicken to find out.

With quick feet, she hurried to the back door. She wasn't sneaking out. She was late for work. And no, it didn't matter that she was her own boss.

After a few gulps of fresh farm air, Romey began to relax. It was another beautiful day in the paradise that was the Verona Commune. There were all the colors of the rainbow as far as the eye could see. Red and green peppers. A field of purple and blue lavender. Orange and yellow gourds.

Weaving amongst the plants were men, women, and children dressed in blue jeans, Indian saris, African Lapa skirts, and orange Hare Krishna robes. Romey greeted everyone in their preferred salutation. Be it a touch of the palm, a kiss to the forehead, or a bow to the divine within them.

Luckily, there were no remarks on the bags under her eyes. Nor any mentions that she was up early for a newlywed. She was able to make it to her lab with very little conversation.

Before entering the converted barn that was her hydroponic garden, Romey put booties over her shoes and pulled gloves on her hands, so as not to attract any outside organisms into her workspace. She opened the door and was greeted by a lush garden in the small place.

Unlike outside, there was no soil inside her lab. Her plants instead grew in coconut fibers or Rockwool, which was another mineral fiber. Though there were acres of land outside these walls, Romey could yield just as much and more in the size of this small barn. Another boon was that her plants grew in a fraction of the time it took for the fledging dealing with the elements outside.

Romey controlled everything in this environment from the water distribution to the amount of daylight her plants got to the nutrients absorbed by the roots. She was the mistress of carbon, water, light, glucose, and oxygen in this realm. Everything necessary for a plant to thrive.

There was no factor that she didn't manipulate in here. No string that she didn't pull, or cut loose, to get the results she wanted. Nothing was introduced into this world that she hadn't planned for.

The exterior door opened, allowing real sunlight and a gust of air in.

"Close the door," she shouted at the intruder.

Paris Montgomery's tall form filled the doorway.

In the soft light of the morning sun, the bags under his eyes shown darker than Romey's. He came just inside the entryway and shut the door behind him.

"You can come in if you put on the protective gear," Romey said.

"This will only take a second," said Paris leaning against the door frame. "I wasn't expecting you to be at work the morning after your wedding. But then I remembered it's you."

"What's that supposed to mean?"

"You've always put this place first, unlike—"

Romey held up her finger to stop the incoming tirade. Paris had been set to marry Jules. However, that had only been his and Romey's plan. Jules had held out for love. And now she was deliriously happy every second of the day. Romey had found it exhausting to watch this last week. Now she couldn't help thinking about how huge her sister smiled any time she was near, or talked about, or was clearly thinking about the man she'd married.

"Looks like your soldier husband and his friends pulled the right strings," said Paris. "The USDA inspector has rescheduled for early next week."

The commune had failed their organic certification inspection last week when the inspector found pesticides on Romey and Jules' soybean crops.

Now that their land was technically no longer apart of the commune, the certification should go through without incident. When it did, that organic stamp of approval would garner the families here a larger profit margin in the markets where they sold their produce.

"That's great," said Romey. "This time, we can get them to swing by here to give a stamp to my hydroponics garden as well."

Paris shuffled his feet on the mat at the door. "Maybe next time. This is all still so new."

"Hydroponics has been around for years, and they're eligible for the organic stamp."

"Romey, let's not make waves. We're on shaky ground as it is. And not everyone is on board with growing food in a lab."

So that's what this was about? Even on her open-minded, everyone is accepted, utopian farmland there were still prejudices. Especially when it came to science.

Well, fine. This was just another problem to solve. If she wasn't going to have the support of her family and friends, then she'd have to substitute another variable to get her hydroponics the approval they deserved.

CHAPTER NINE

*T*he sound of artillery fire filled Spinelli's ears. The grunts and groans of war mixed with gunshots and explosives banged out from the speakers. Flashes and bursts of pixels colored the monitors arrayed on the desks as the heat signatures of soldiers moved around the field of play.

"Rogue Five, can you identify whether the target is hostile?" shouted the unit leader.

"Negative, sir. Identity unclear," was the response.

Spinelli smiled behind his steepled fingers as he watched the game play out on the screens. The first objective of his war game simulation, Tactical Approach, was about identifying the enemy. Players were trapped in darkness, unable to see whether they faced a uniformed soldier, an innocent civilian, or an enemy hiding in plain sight. They would have to rely on logic to smoke out any adversaries by using patterns that would reveal hostility. Because these soldiers were trained mostly with sight, they were losing points.

Another round of fire lit up the speakers in the control room. A high pitched wail signaled friendly fire had taken out yet another team member.

"I'm hit," called the downed man. He'd only lost his life on the game board and not in reality. Still, it was a blow to the team.

Spinelli winced when the remaining soldiers came up against more hostiles dressed in plain clothes. What would they do? They had a myriad of options. Spinelli knew what he would do, but he'd designed the game, so he remained tight-lipped.

"Hold your fire," shouted the team leader.

But the man's voice was drowned out by more sounds of artillery. This time coming from their opponents in the game. The algorithms Spinelli had designed had learned the lessons the soldiers hadn't. The enemy had picked up the patterns of the soldiers' movements, clearly identifying their targets and taking them out one by one.

Spinelli turned to Rusty, who sat to his right. Instead of seeing a grin on his friend's face, Rusty was grimacing and pinching at his brow as he watched the massacre on screen. Spinelli couldn't reason why? The coding he'd programmed had worked brilliantly. The objective had been met, albeit by the enemy and not the self-appointed good guys.

On Spinelli's other side sat Commander Jackson South. Commander South watched his team of elite soldiers on the screen. His brows were drawn as though deep in thought. His mouth was a straight line that left no room for interpretation.

Smiles, Spinelli could identify. Frowns, he understood. Anything in between, Spinelli had trouble with.

He was much better at watching people's actions and predicting future movements. Spinelli's prediction was that the Commander would love his simulation and the challenges it presented his men. He would then sign on for full training, thus bringing in another client for the Boots on the Ground Training camp he and his friends had created.

While the others worked outside on the obstacle courses and drilling, Spinelli had built a state of the art virtual war games arena. He'd been a gamer all his life since his parents had handed him their cell phone as a toddler to keep him quiet. He quickly went through Solitaire and Chess at age two. By age five, he'd mastered every game available on the Gameboy. By his teen years, he'd grown bored with Nintendo and Xbox.

It wasn't until he'd come into contact with a commercial version of a war game known as Full Spectrum Warrior that he'd found a challenge. It took him weeks to beat it. And then he'd hacked the code to play the official, top-secret Army version. Playing that game day and night, Spinelli had come to a life-changing revelation. He'd put down his controller and signed up for JROTC, determined to become a real-life soldier.

Basic training had been a nightmare as his scrawny arm and leg muscles, which had only ever lifted a game controller, strained under the demand. With the hard work and dedication that he'd shown to his gaming and coding escapades, his geeky body had eventually filled out. He'd seen his fair share of combat while enlisted. It was nothing like the games he'd played. That's why he strove to make Tactical Approach fully realistic.

Out in the theater of war, it was difficult to tell

the good guys from the bad guys. That and another dozen decisions came at soldiers every single day. Sometimes every hour as they strove to follow orders, complete their mission, and simply survive.

More shouts came from the console, breaking Spinelli's walk down a digital memory lane. The remaining soldiers were backed into a corner and still unable to tell who was friendly and who was the enemy. The unit leader gave the call to surrender. The game was over. For now.

Lights illuminated the game arena, which was nothing more than a large room with pillars for the players to maneuver around or find cover. The men tore off their virtual headgear in frustration. Commander South sat back in his chair with a sigh.

He pursed his lips as he regarded Spinelli. That wasn't a frown. Nor was it a smile. But the man did look pensive. That had to be a good sign. Spinelli decided not to try and interpret. Instead, he began spouting facts, as he wished others would do.

"As you see, the game is realistic," Spinelli began.

"That it is," said the Commander. "The realism is uncanny."

Spinelli let his lips raise in a smile at the compliment. He looked to Rusty to share his good cheer. The man wasn't smiling. He still pinched the skin at his temple, a look Spinelli had seen the hostage negotiator wear when things were not going his way.

"The weapons, the equipment," Commander South continued. "You even put language and cultural nuances into the simulation."

Spinelli had worked hard on all those details. There had been times when making the right gesture while in a hostile zone had saved his life. Any soldier coming into the training facility needed to take all of these things into account for when they went out into the true field of combat.

Commander South slapped his hands down on the console table. "This is not what we're looking for."

Spinelli's head did a comical double-take. Had he heard the Commander right? Had the man said Spinelli's realistic scenarios weren't what he was looking for to prepare his team?

"This is an unwinnable scenario you've crafted here," said Commander South.

"No, it's winnable," said Spinelli. "The men just need to prepare for the eventualities."

"There are tons of eventualities in the real world," said the Commander. "No man could prepare for them all."

Spinelli begged to differ. He could. And when he'd fallen short, he'd added the missed eventuality to his memory bank. All of that knowledge he'd downloaded into this simulation. It was designed to prepare soldiers for every possibility they might be faced with.

"Only a computer could keep all of that intel straight," Commander South was saying.

Spinelli's friends often called him the Cyborg, likening his memory as well as his motions and emotions to that of a computer interface. He knew it was meant to be a joke. But he'd never figured out the funny part.

"They need to be challenged to become better," he said in response to the commander.

"Challenge, yes. Knocked down until they cry uncle, no. I'll tell you what? If there is a different level, one where success is an option, we'll give it another go."

A dumbed-down version? That was a recipe to get people killed. Spinelli wanted to prepare these men and women for whatever may come.

"We'll change out the program and have you and your team visit another day." That came from Rusty. The man was using his reasonable voice, the same voice he used to talk a suicide bomber into taking their thumb off the detonator.

Once again, the voice worked. Commander South gave the two of them a nod. Spinelli managed a nod in return as Rusty walked the man out of the door. Spinelli knew his team needed this contract. But he had no idea how he was going to dumb his game down. He didn't even have the desire to. The only desire he had was to go home and rest his head.

That idea perked him up. If he did go home, his wife would be there. His partner. She'd vowed to listen to him as part of their marriage. Romey was brilliant. Maybe she could help him solve this problem.

CHAPTER TEN

*R*omey inhaled deeply under the late afternoon sun. Clouds moved overhead, casting her in shadow as she looked off in the distance. Twenty feet away stood a colorful target with a green bull's eye. The target was mostly used for archery practice, but Romey had a different use for it today.

She squared her shoulders. With another inhale, she checked the alignment of her spine, visualizing that each disc of her spine was stacked perfectly straight, one on top of the other. It was a trick she'd learned during meditation class as a child.

With another inhale, she raised her right arm. Again, she made sure that her shoulder made a straight line to her index finger, where she held a gun. She took a moment to muse that meditation and guns didn't go hand in hand before she used her thumb to flick off the safety.

Sighting the target in the distance, under a copse of trees, she squeezed the trigger slowly until... BANG.

The feel of the recoil was satisfying. The *thwap* of the bullet hitting its green mark was gratifying. After Paris's easy dismissal of her efforts to get her hydroponic garden certified, she'd felt her anger boiling up until it was ready to explode.

Romey didn't like to feel out of control. She certainly didn't want to hug it out in an Empathy Circle. She wanted to hit something. The target was her best bet.

She decided to make it a little harder and give herself a challenge. Lowering her weapon, she stepped back a few paces. And promptly bumped into a solid mass of muscle.

Romey whirled around. But it was the gun that made it there first. She'd pulled her finger off the trigger, knowing that there would be no foe on her land.

She needn't have worried about the gun going off. The weapon was quickly stripped from her hand. Jordan expertly checked the chamber before flicking the safety back on.

"I didn't know flower children played with guns," he said. "Or with real bullets. I remember seeing a hippie putting a flower in the barrel of a gun."

"We have no issues with the second amendment here."

The clouds chose that moment to part and cast Jordan Spinelli in its full glow. The grin that spread across his face made him look like one of the stars on the posters of the town movie theater. The man was devastatingly attractive.

How had Romey ended up with a man so beautiful? She'd always expected she would end up with a smart guy. A nerdy science teacher. Jordan was smart and handsome, and he liked her for her mind.

Meanwhile, she couldn't stop thinking about what it had been like to kiss him the other day. What would it be like to kiss him today? Out in the field, where no one would see.

There was a sheen of sweat on his cheek. Would the salt of his sweat alter the sweetness of his breath? Or would that little droplet make him all the more savory?

"Romey?"

"Yes?" Oh no, he'd been talking. What had he been saying? He held the disabled gun out to her. "I wasn't going to shoot you."

"I know. I saw that you'd lowered your arm. But old habits die hard."

Spinelli sighed as he looked down at the gun. His head cocked to the side, much like the motion of putting the safety on. But the expression on his face made Romey wonder if he wanted to flick the safety back off.

"Mind if I...?" He made a motion to the gun she cradled in her palm.

"Of course not." Romey handed the gun back to him. "You just have to stay on this track so that the bullets don't get into the field."

Jordan flicked off the safety. He squared his shoulders and eyed the target. Romey didn't hear him taking a breath, but she saw his chest rise before he pulled the trigger. His shoulders bunched at the recoil, causing Romey to let out a small gasp at the play of muscles there.

Again, she gave herself a shake, trying to loose these errant thoughts of objectification about her brilliant husband, who just so happened to have a few attractive qualities. He had a brain. And so did she.

"You know," she said, "I had this idea for environmentally friendly ammunition that biodegrades."

"Really?" Jordan turned back to her. Weapon lowered, target forgotten as she told him more about her idea.

"Yes, well, you know that most bullets are made of lead."

Jordan nodded. "There was a push for more copper-based bullets, which are less toxic to the environment."

"I read that. But what if we made bullets that were not only non-toxic but environmentally friendly. Where the material would turn to seeds and germinate... after... you know."

"After the circle of life, you mean?"

He flashed her another of those grins. Under his perusal, Romey had the oddest inclination. She reached for a lock of her overgrown hair and began twirling it around her finger. Jordan's gaze slid to the movement of her fingers, playing with her hair. After a moment, his eyes slid to her face.

"You're brilliant," he said. Then he cleared his throat. "I mean, the idea is brilliant."

"Thanks."

He swallowed a few times, his throat working as

though he was having trouble moving past a lump there. Finally, he turned back to the target, aimed, and fired. His form was magnificent, his aim perfect, but somehow he missed the target. The bullet lodged into one of the surrounding trees.

"I hope that wasn't an ancient, protected tree," he said.

"It's a mistletoe tree. Placing the bullseye here was the parent's way to keep their kids from sneaking off and necking here."

Jordan's brows rose as he looked up at the bloom-less tree. Romey was about to tell him that the tree only bloomed its noteworthy berries during the winter season. But then a branch fell off a nearby tree. A slight wind blew the tumbleweed forward until it rested at their feet.

Romey and Jordan stared down at the berry-less branch. It wasn't as though she believed in superstitions. She was a woman of science. She didn't fret over stepping on a crack, especially not when she had to get to where she was going. It was pretty difficult to not walk under a ladder while repairing a structure. There were tons of affectionate black cats all over this farm who brightened her days.

So, no, she was not at all affected by a branch of mistletoe rolling at her feet. Unless Jordan was?

Romey chanced a glance up at the man. Jordan frowned down at the branch. Then he lifted his gaze.

"I didn't know those trees could grow here," he said.

"Mama Lily can get anything to grow anywhere," Romey said with a touch of pride in her voice. Their resident herb lady had been instrumental in Romey's upbringing in the world of botany.

Jordan nodded, stealing another glance at the wayward branch. Then back at her. "Is your workday over?"

"Yes." Romey nodded, looking away from the branch as it rolled over their feet. "Yours?"

"Thankfully."

"Bad day?"

"Let's just say it didn't go as I planned it."

"Me, too."

"Should we honor our vows and talk about it?"

"I think that would be an acceptable use of our time."

Now back on footing she understood, Romey walked in step with her husband. Things were getting back on track. She glanced over her shoulder and saw that the mistletoe was following their footsteps. The funny thing was, there was no longer a breeze.

CHAPTER ELEVEN

At the end of their wedding yesterday, Spinelli and Romey had crossed the threshold of their home and retreated to their respective rooms. He'd missed her on his way to work this morning. Having her beside him in the kitchen, listening to her relay her day of working in her hydroponic garden left him feeling... full.

He had no other word for the feeling. His mind was engaged in the explanation of her work. His ears were hooked on the sounds of her voice. His eyes were pinned to the movement of her lips.

"Do you see what I'm saying?"

Spinelli swallowed, and then blinked a couple of times. "Yes, yes. Clearly."

"I knew you'd understand," she smiled up at him.

He would understand. If he had heard a single word she'd said, he might have. But he hadn't.

What he did understand was her smile. It clearly said that she was pleased with him. He liked pleasing her. He racked his brain to say something else to please her. But he couldn't think of a single thing. Just the mere sight of the woman and Spinelli slipped into a trance.

"This sauce smells divine," said Romey, bending over the pot of fresh chopped tomatoes simmering in a pan, but not daring to touch it.

They'd picked the tomatoes straight off the vines as they made their way back to their house. Not off any of the vines outside. Romey had taken him into her hydroponic garden. He'd heard her talk about her greenhouse laboratory. This had been the first time she'd let him inside her sanctuary.

Spinelli had been astounded at the sight. Not only was his wife beautiful, and intelligent, she was inventive. Dare he say, magical. He'd never heard of growing plants without soil. But Romey had done it.

They'd only stopped in briefly to gather a few ingredients for their dinner, but he'd wanted to stay longer. He'd have to invite himself back later.

Especially if he got to see her eyes light up like they had at his questions over her methods and procedures.

There was so much he didn't know about this woman, his wife. She was a great shot. She could grow anything right out of thin air. And she boiled a mean pot of water. Though if left unattended, she would've likely burned the spaghetti. Fortunately, her one imperfection, being wholly unable to cook, didn't tarnish any of her shine.

"I'm part Italian." Spinelli emptied the noodles he'd rescued into a strainer in the sink. "Can't grow up without knowing how to make sauce from scratch."

"My father's family was from the south, they cooked everything in some kind of pig fat or with a pig's appendage."

From outside the door, Hamlet, their pet pig, squealed. Spinelli didn't think the pig was indignant at his extended family's dietary habits. Hamlet knew he was safe on this commune of vegans. No, the pig was irate about not being let inside.

When Porco and Spinelli had moved in earlier this week, they had both scoffed at the pig being inside of doors. Jules had put her foot down. With three against one, the pig had been relegated outside where it belonged.

"My mom was raised with maids and cooks," Romey continued, ignoring Hamlet's pleas. "Something she rebelled against in her youth, though I wouldn't have minded much. Either way, I got no training in the kitchen other than to pick what I wanted to eat from the ground, rub off the dirt, and pop it into my mouth."

That said, she rubbed a ripe tomato on her shirt and took a bite. Spinelli was far more interested in her shirt. It featured a cat carrying a large bone. *I found this humerus*, said the caption bubble over the cat. Spinelli chuckled. Finally, a joke he understood.

"Hey," Spinelli admonished, as Romey took another bite of the tomato. "You'll spoil your dinner."

She giggled at him but set the tomato down. Spinelli was left to ponder why that trickle of laughter left him feeling warmth across his shoulders. Sound shouldn't have that power. But already, he'd gotten lost at the sound of her voice. He'd become entranced by her words. So it would stand to reason that her laugh would warm him.

Earlier when the mistletoe had landed between them, Spinelli had frowned down at it, wishing it had somehow hung over their heads. He knew the social obligations that standing under a mistletoe imbued. He would've been bound to kiss her. But it lay on the ground and then rolled away.

Romey turned from him. She sliced off the piece of tomato she'd bitten and begun chopping the rest. With that done, she tossed the juicy bits of tomato into a salad. The leafy greens were also from her hydroponic garden. The only thing she hadn't grown was the pasta.

"I actually didn't like spaghetti until I saw the movie *The Lady and the Tramp*," said Romey.

"I know that movie," said Spinelli. "I saw it when I was a kid. Though it took me a couple of views to accept that cartoon animals could talk."

Romey giggled again.

Spinelli wasn't sure what the joke was. If he could figure it out, he'd say it again. "I take it you're referring to the spaghetti scene? The part where they share the same noodle?"

"Yes, that part."

"It's highly unlikely for a strand to be that long."

"Yes, I know. It was all nonsensical. But it was cute."

Spinelli agreed. He dumped the cooked pasta out of the strainer and into a serving dish. With a ladle, he spooned the sauce over the noodles.

"You listened as I shared the woes of my day," said Romey, taking her seat. "By our vow of the Michelangelo Phenomenon, I'm bound to listen to yours."

Spinelli chewed at the inside of his lip as he twirled pasta onto his fork.

"Vows aside, I want you to tell me," Romey said. "Maybe I can help you think it through and come to a solution."

Spinelli smiled at that. There were no ambiguities with this woman. She said what she meant and meant what she said. He reaffirmed that he would tamp down these irrational feelings of wanting to kiss her and give her what she'd asked for; a rational man who was her intellectual equal.

"I built a simulation; a war game. The client said it was too difficult for his team, that they couldn't possibly prepare for the challenges I created. But I believe soldiers need to prepare for every eventuality."

Romey nodded, eyes intent on him as she chewed her noodles. There was a dollop of sauce lingering at the corner of her mouth. Spinelli averted his gaze from the temptation to wipe, or daresay lick, it off.

"War doesn't happen in a controlled

environment," he went on. "I don't want to dumb it down in my simulations."

"Is the scenario winnable?" Romey asked.

"Yes, if you prepare."

"So, it's not a Kobayashi Maru?"

"No." Spinelli grinned at the *Star Trek* reference to the unwinnable training exercise that every Starfleet Academy cadet was put through. "It's not a no-win scenario."

"But it would take a Spock to figure it out?" She waved her fork at him as though he'd been naughty. "Not everyone is as smart as you, Jordan. You know that, right?"

He liked that she called him Jordan. Having been in the military for the last five years, he rarely heard his first name. It made him feel human. Especially with a group of friends that casually and jokingly referred to him as a cyborg.

He also liked that she thought he was smart. Even more, he liked showing this woman that he was smart. He'd show her that he was smart enough to figure out how to make Tactical Approach less high-level Spock and more winnable Kirk.

"This sauce is delicious," she said as she reached for another helping of the pasta dish.

Spinelli looked down to see that his fork was in

the dish as well. He pulled his fork back. There was already a strand of spaghetti wrapped around his tines. It was a long strand that stretched from his fork all the way to hers.

Spinelli grinned at the thought of the Lady and her Tramp of a dinner partner. When he looked up, he saw that Romey grinned as though she were thinking the same thing.

Then her gaze dipped to his lips. His lips parted, no longer interested in a second helping of pasta. He wanted a huge helping of Romey. But she was pushing back from the table.

"You know what?" She stood up, her chair legs scraping on the hardwood floors. "I'm full."

Without another word, she dashed from the kitchen. Moments later, Spinelli heard the shower going.

Great. He'd gone and bungled it. She had to have guessed that his mind wasn't on their discussion of his work. She had to have seen that all he was thinking about was his carnal desires, and he had no way of hiding that fact from her. Suddenly this felt like the ultimate Kobayashi Maru scenario. He had no idea how he would win in this marriage.

CHAPTER TWELVE

*W*aking was a struggle the next morning. Romey's dreams kept pulling her back under their warm covers. Part of her knew she was dreaming, but the lines kept getting fuzzier and fuzzier until they became furry.

She was panting in the dream. Her tongue lolled out of her mouth. She was down on all fours, trotting about a back alley. Distressed that she'd get her beautiful brown coat of fur messy. Why did she have paws in her dreams? Why was she sniffing after a scruffy looking gray and white dog with a lopsided grin? Why was she hankering for a meatball?

Romey woke with a start. Her heart was racing. There was drool on her lips. Thankfully her tongue was snug inside her mouth. Her skin was clean, with no hint of fur.

Sigmund Freud had a theory of dreams. The psychologist had postulated that dreams represented an individual's unconscious dreams and desires. They were wish fulfillments behind closed lids. Motivations acted upon in the dark recesses of the mind.

So, did that mean Romey wanted to be a dog? Ridiculous as it sounded, it was better than admitting to the other thing. That she desperately wanted to kiss her husband.

There was another theory of dreams. One where it was postulated that the neuropathways of our brains used the downtime to sort through problems and events of the day that still required our attention. But how did her dream of being Lady make any sense? Jordan was definitely the beautiful coated dog in real life, and she was the tramp who played in the mud all day.

Throwing off the covers, Romey stood. She shook her limbs, trying to shake out the last vestiges of the dream. None of it mattered. It was a new day, and she was going to spend it living up to the vows she'd made with and to her husband.

She dressed quickly, pulling on a black T-shirt

that best reflected her mood. On the shirt was a rat outlined in white. Above him, the thought bubble red *Science experiments are fun*. Whenever her family and friends on the commune saw the shirt, they pursed their lips and shook their heads. Everyone was far too emotional to get the joke.

Before leaving her room, Romey pressed her ear to the door. The house was quiet. Jules and David still hadn't returned from their impromptu honeymoon. Romey was sad about it. She needed a glance at her head-in-the-clouds sister to remind herself why she kept her feet firmly on the ground.

Twice yesterday, she and Jordan had been put in situations as though the universe was trying to get them to kiss. Which was ridiculous. Romey believed in God, but she doubted that the entity had any time to design her love life. That was simply preposterous, with the wars, and famine, and strife in the world. God wouldn't be paying attention to her happiness. The entity was far too busy.

If her sister were to tell it, Jules would say that God was love, and that was the deity's primary task. Romey simply couldn't get behind the idea that the creator of all the complex, numerical, symmetry of the world would give a single care over whether or not she and her husband touched lips.

But she couldn't deny the coincidences. As a scientist, she didn't believe in random acts. Everything was served a purpose.

With her ear pressed to the door, Romey heard the patter of size twelve footfalls in the hall. Jordan was up. Sure enough, the patter of water falling in the shower sounded next.

Romey closed her eyes, trying to shut out any imaginings of the man under the spout. Behind her eyes, her imagination, which usually lent itself to growth patterns in nature, went wild.

She imagined the droplets running off his chest. She imagined the suds gathering on his strong biceps. She imagined Jordan lifting his face to the spray and the water raining down on those beautiful lips of his and-

Romey shook herself. She had to get control over herself. This wasn't the type of marriage either of them had signed up for. She was not the kind of woman who men went romantic over. There would be no sweeping of any feet.

Her feet were on the ground, where they belonged. She stood on steady legs. She had work to do. With her resolve in place, she slipped out of her bedroom door -quickly. She didn't want to run into her husband after he got out of the shower.

She left the house so fast, she didn't bother with breakfast or the lunch of leftover spaghetti she'd packed last night. She'd grab something from a vine or tree on her way. She did just that, grabbing a tomato from a vine, she took a bite. But the fresh fruit paled in comparison to the sauce Jordan had made last night.

Still, she needed sustenance for her long day. Her morning would be spent helping the commune kids with their science projects for the town science fair. She'd have to be on her toes with this bunch. They'd been allowed the freedom to run wild and think radically. She wouldn't be surprised if Cinnamon Fairchild was trying to make a time machine to stop all the world's dictators from being born. Nor would Romey be surprised if the device actually worked given the IQ of the girl.

When Romey walked into the schoolroom, she didn't find the kids working on their world-changing science projects. No, she found them behaving like normal, hormone riddled teenagers.

A group of girls and boys stood gathered around a table. The magnifying glasses were moved to the side. There was a bottle at the center of the table. It was spinning.

"Cinnamon, Zion, Winter, Falcon, and Archer, what are you all up to?"

But Romey could guess. They were preteens. They were curious. And the resident midwife had given them all the facts about their reproductive health and how things worked.

Though these kids were allowed to run wild and think freely, they each had a healthy respect for authority and consequences. They all jumped back from the spinning bottle and looked away from Romey's glare. Before Romey could launch in on them about the commune's rule of having anyone under the age of eighteen have a sit-down dinner with both the families before engaging in any type of sexual exploration, the door to the school opened behind her.

Great. Now she would be dragged into the family conversations since the non-sanctioned kissing game was being played on her watch. Romey had no desire to have another talk about birds and bees and the *Kama Sutra*. Her first talk at twelve had left her scared and scarred.

But it was too late. The door opened behind them. Romey looked up to see Jordan in the entryway. He was freshly showered and shaved. He was decked out in a plain, green T-shirt, fatigue pants, and heavy boots. The man was simply stunning. So stunning that Romey's breath caught in her throat.

"Hey," he said.

"Hey," she managed.

"They said I'd find you in here. You forgot your lunch."

Jordan strode toward her. Romey felt her knees weaken as she watched him move. Her own hormones were going haywire inside her blood. As he stretched his hand toward her to hand her her lunch, Romey nicked the neck bottle at the center of the table and set it spinning again.

Round and round the glass went. The children stepped back up to the table to watch. Everyone held their breath as its spinning began to slow. When the bottle stopped, the top landed facing her. The bottom faced Jordan.

Jordan's lips parted. He spoke a soundless word that Romey couldn't make out. Then his gaze rose to hers. He closed his mouth and swallowed hard.

Did he notice? Was he keeping track? This was the third time they had been put in a situation where convention would lead them to kiss. This was no coincidence. God, the universe, some mathematical force wanted her and her husband to lock lips.

Maybe they should? All in the name of science, of course. It could be an experiment. To try to determine what was going on.

Jordan cleared his throat. This time his words were spoken loud and clear. "Enjoy your lesson, kids. I'll see you later at home, Romey."

He sat the bag down next to the bottle. He turned on his heel, and like the soldier he was, he marched out the door.

Romey swallowed her disappointment. She picked up the bottle and tossed it into the recycling bin. Then she directed each kid to their own table and set them to work on their projects. With that done, Romey stepped out for some much needed fresh air.

When next she saw her husband, Romey was determined to have a logical, rational talk with him about these coincidences that kept occurring, and what they were going to do about it. Because she was certain it would happen again, and she was tired of fighting the inevitability.

CHAPTER THIRTEEN

*T*he cold water from the tap rained down on Spinelli's body. He turned the shower dial towards the blue letter C. The ice that came from the shower head wasn't enough to cool him down.

He'd taken a cold shower before he'd fallen into a restless night of sleep after the meatball fiasco. Even when he'd closed his eyes, thoughts of Romey with red tomato sauce coating her mouth, assaulted him. He could not get the thought of kissing his wife out of his mind.

Why had he told her about *The Lady and the Tramp*? He hadn't thought of that movie in years. And what were the odds that after telling her about the spaghetti scene that he'd unravel the world's longest strand of spaghetti, which if they'd been slurping up with their mouths instead of forks, would've led them to kiss just like the cartoon canines in the film.

There was the spaghetti. Then there had been the mistletoe that had fallen between them. And now the pubescent game of spin the bottle. If Spinelli weren't a logical man, he'd swear that everything in the natural and animated world was pushing him towards kissing his wife.

So why was he resisting?

He'd wanted to pull Romey close since the first moment he'd laid eyes on her and seen that intelligent gaze. Eyes that showed they clearly understood him without the need of any dumbing down of his words. Spinelli could be himself with her. No hiding. No changing. Romey got him. And he got her.

Except for this one aspect of their lives together.

He'd been drawn to her that first day in the grocery store. He'd known he'd wanted to get closer to her the more she spoke. That night, he'd hated being parted from her. She was the first thing he'd thought about the next day when he'd woken up. And every day after.

The facts were all there as clear as the pattern of

a Fibonacci sequence. The sequence of events showed a clear pattern. The math unraveled to show a simple equation.

Jordan had fallen in love with his wife the first time he'd laid eyes on her. The answer was there in that first meeting. But because he hadn't given voice two the elegant solution, it kept repeating itself. Each interaction after the first was the sum of the previous two interactions, increasing the answer and shining a golden light on the outcome.

It was all so simple. It was love. He let out a laugh at the thought. Water droplets filled his mouth. He didn't spit out the liquid, he swallowed it down like the truth.

So, what did this mean for their marriage and the vows they'd made to each other?

He and Romey had experienced a meeting of the minds in the short time that they'd known each other. But he wanted more. He wanted a meeting in the physical realm. But did she?

He wasn't sure. He'd never been good at reading the emotions of other people. Let alone, the emotions of the opposite sex.

What if she didn't want anything more with him other than what was in their vows? At the end of the day, was a physical relationship required if one found the person who was their match in every other way? He wanted to kiss Romey, and more. But he simply wanted to be in her presence more than anything.

He knew he needed to manage this. This was not the marriage either of them had designed. He couldn't go to her and change the terms so soon. Maybe in a couple of years, he could ask for a reevaluation of their terms.

Spinelli toweled off for the second time this morning. He'd left his clothes back in his bedroom. Since the house was empty, he wrapped the towel at his hips and pulled open the bathroom door. He stepped out of the bathroom and walked directly into Romey.

Her gaze was fastened on the droplets, still streaming off his chest. Was it his imagination, or did her nostrils flare? Was he dreaming, or did she just bite at her bottom lip? Those were signs of arousal, weren't they?

"Hello," she said.

"Hi."

They stared. The sounds of their shallow breathing filled his ears. Spinelli swore he felt an electric spark in the air between them. He was long past denying that the rules of science no longer applied when it came to this woman. From the first moment he'd seen her, he'd felt charged just by being in her presence.

"I'm sorry," he said. "I'll just get dressed."

"Don't."

Romey put up a hand to stop him. Her hand was between them, her palm just a breath from his beating heart. Her fingers curled in and lightly brushed his chest. Spinelli inhaled as though her five fingertips were matches, and she'd struck his skin. He had to look down to be sure she didn't leave a heat trail.

"You are so symmetrical," she said, her fingers tracing over his pecks.

Spinelli held himself entirely still. He was certain now that she was leaving a trail. His skin burned with her light touch. The burning sensation was good. He wanted more.

"It's like you were sculpted from clay," she breathed.

"I work out," he said by way of explanation because Romey liked it when he explained his process. "I used to be scrawny because I only played video games. When I got into the army, I worked hard for this physique."

"It shows." She took a deep breath and blew it out.

The heat of her breath made his insides warm. Spinelli couldn't take it any longer. He captured her hand in his.

That was a mistake. It brought them closer together. All he needed to do was dip his head down and capture her lips. Not in the few years he'd planned, but in the next few seconds.

"Listen," she said, linking her fingers with his, "you need to know that I find you very attractive. It's a simple biological reaction as you are perfectly proportioned to showcase to a female that you can provide for her, protect her, and... procreate."

Now it was Spinelli who let out a low breath. He urged himself to focus on her words. He wasn't one given to much imagination. But the words coming from her lips were giving him ideas of showing Romey what he could do with his perfectly proportioned body.

"I find you perfectly symmetrical as well," he said. "The way your eyes lift at the corners makes me want to measure the angle. I'd bet the distance between your limbs is perfectly ratioed as well. You're like a walking Golden Ratio."

The eyes he admired so much lifted higher at the

corners. As did her lips. Romey grinned up at him as though she were delighted.

"Did you just compare me to a Fibonacci sequence?" she said.

"I did."

"That's the nicest compliment anyone has ever given to me."

"You're mathematically perfect," he said.

Her smile dimmed. "Mathematically?"

Spinelli got the sense that something wasn't adding up. She'd said his words were a compliment. So why was she frowning now?

"Mathematically. Of course." Romey tugged at her hand until Spinelli freed her fingers. She pulled away from him, no longer meeting his gaze.

Spinelli wanted to reach out and tilt her head up so that he could see directly into her eyes. Hers was the only gaze that he could get any read on. For the past week, she'd been telling him exactly what was on her mind. She was silent now.

"Did I say something wrong?" he asked.

"No." She shook her head. "No, you made things between us perfectly clear."

Romey gave Spinelli a tight smile, and then she turned on her heel and left. Spinelli stared after her for a long moment. He had no idea what had just happened, but it hadn't ended the way he wanted. He ripped off the towel, shoved into his clothes, and raced after her. He was no longer the master of his mind. His feelings had taken over, and he was glad of it.

CHAPTER FOURTEEN

*R*omey's cheeks were heated as she stepped into the cool enclosure of her hydroponic garden. She put her hands to her cheeks. She couldn't see the redness on her face, but her skin certainly was warm enough to indicate that she was blushing. Despite being a darker tone of skin, her flesh was just creamy enough to redden.

Romey couldn't exactly blame it on her mother. Despite her fair skin, Mariam Capulano never blushed. The woman was fearless. Mariam had tried to join the Black Panther Party...as a white woman. It was her mother that had taught Romey to shoot, that had taught her to never back down to injustice, and to believe in her principles.

It was Romey's father who had taught her that she did have a romantic side. Jerome Capulano had loved the Victorian classics. Despite Romey's best efforts, some of those romantic notions had penetrated her consciousness.

She remembered reading many books where pale-skinned damsels blushed over their knights in armor as they spouted bad poetry up to a balcony window. Romey hadn't blushed when she'd stood toe to toe with her knight, who hadn't been wearing a stitch of armor. She hadn't blushed when she'd made her play for Jordan by telling him how attractive she'd found him. She'd had her wits about her then, but somehow it had all gone wrong when he'd gone and called her mathematically perfect.

In all the Shakespearean plays and sonnets, Romey didn't remember any hero comparing their true love to a math problem. No, those girls got compared to summer days, the winds, and buds in May. With such compliments, it was no wonder that the blood raced to their cheeks to show their affections.

Romey's cheeks flushed now in the privacy of her inner sanctum. Just thinking back over her actions with her husband made her cringe.

Had she really run her hands over Jordan's chest? Had she really told him that he was symmetrical and perfectly proportioned? When she thought about it, her compliments were just as bad as his.

But what had she expected? Romance from two people who had professed to be too logical to believe in such flowery nonsense?

It was just that Romey wasn't so sure it was nonsense anymore.

She had to admit to herself that she did harbor a fantasy of a man falling for her. She did harbor a fantasy of a man sweeping her off her feet. She did harbor hope that she might experience that indefinable notion of true love.

Well, she was experiencing it. There was no other conclusion to draw from the way her heart skipped a beat when she was near Jordan. It wasn't a medical condition. It was attraction. It was desire. And she had no idea how to deal with it. Not within herself. Not to determine if the feeling was there in her husband.

If she confronted him again about her feelings, it would likely dissolve into another think tank on the inner workings of the ventricular system or the rate that the synapses in the brain fired. She didn't know how to talk of love. Which was a hoot, because she could talk about any subject matter. But this—this elusive idea of love—she hadn't the first clue on where to set foot.

The door of the barn opened. In the doorway stood Jordan. His perfectly proportioned figure filled the entire frame. He glanced at her, a fierce determination in his gaze. He took a stride toward her, his heavy boots thudding as they impacted the ground.

"Wait!" Romey held up her hands. "You'll contaminate the plants."

Her brain might be scrambled. But not enough to forsake safety measures for her garden. She might be letting errant thoughts run amok in her mind, but no contaminations would get inside this carefully regulated environment.

Jordan stopped in his tracks. He turned to the sanitation station just inside the door. He bent his large form down to put booties on his boots and gloves on his hands. Once sterile, he resumed his mission toward her.

"I need you to explain it to me," he said.

"Explain what?"

"I called you beautiful, and you ran away from me."

Romey's mouth worked, but no sound came out on the first try. She had the same result with the second try. Finally, she cleared her throat and tried again.

"You didn't call me beautiful. You said I was mathematically perfect."

"That's my idea of beauty. An equation that is both complex and simple. Elegant in the way it balances variables. Challenging yet clear in its expression."

Oh. Well. When he put it like that—take that you summer day girls. She was a complex, elegant, expressive variable.

"That's my idea of beauty." Jordan stepped closer to her.

The distance between them was so slight that she'd need the millimeter side of a ruler to calculate it. Not inches. "It appears that we both find each other physically pleasing, based on our biological responses. Which is completely natural in the animal kingdom."

"Completely natural," Jordan agreed.

"There's also the legal pull as we're married," Romey went on.

"That we are."

They were also now in centimeter territory in the

closeness category. Though, in truth, Romey had lost the train of the conversation. All she could see were the lines of Jordan's lower lip. She wanted to trace them to see if there was any pattern to the design.

"When we agreed to get married, we outlined a well-informed, heavily referenced, fact-checked agreement," Jordan said. "I want to toss our marital agreement aside."

Romey's heart sank. Did he want a divorce? Or, more likely, an annulment. He could have that as they'd never consummated the marriage. It would be the cleanest way to get it done.

"I need more," he said. "We're going to have to renegotiate."

"Renegotiate?"

"Yes. There are additional items I'd like to add to this marriage project."

Romey's head was spinning. Was he asking to terminate their marriage or...?

"The first item is kissing."

"Kissing?" She realized she was parroting the man, but her brain was malfunctioning. She was scrambling for any scrap of understanding.

"I want to kiss you," said Jordan.

Well, that was clear. "You do? Now?"

"Yes," he said.

They were still standing within a breath's distance of one another, but they weren't touching.

"Yes, now," Jordan continued. "Then later. I'd like to kiss you a lot."

That was exactly what Romey wanted. She wanted to reach out to him right now and get started. But she was feeling dizzy, lightheaded. For the life of her, her brain couldn't remember how to move a limb. It was too focused on breathing in and out and not taking her eyes off the beautiful man standing before her.

"I'm open to negotiating the amount," Jordan was saying. "If that would make you comfortable."

"A lot is a good amount. I would agree to that term."

"A lot is not a very specific number," he said. "We should probably quantify it, for clarity."

"Or, we could just leave it open to interpretation."

Jordan frowned, as though he didn't comprehend the notion. Before Romey could take it back, the corner of his mouth lifted. The grin that spread across his lips told Romey that, not only did he get it, he wanted the stipulation.

"So," Jordan said, "we're going to do this? We're going to kiss?"

Romey tugged her upper lip into her mouth. She

quickly moistened it before doing the same with her lower lip. She desperately wanted to breathe into the cup of her palm and do a smell test, but there was no time. The centimeter of space between them was reduced to the nanoscale.

And then... impact.

CHAPTER FIFTEEN

Spinelli placed his index finger under Romey's chin. Tilting her face up toward him, he took a moment to appreciate the slant of the obtuse angle from her jawline to her chin. He wanted to tell her about the geometry he was seeing in her. But he decided against it.

His first overture with the mathematical perfection of his wife hadn't gone so well. He needed this moment to be perfect, not just for her, but for him as well. Because he'd meant what he'd said.

He planned to kiss his wife a lot. Though they hadn't determined an exact quantity, he had an amount in mind. The number was far too large to encapsulate on a sheet of graph paper.

Looking down at the woman in his care, Spinelli felt a sense of possessiveness come over him. All logic and reason left his mind. He'd vowed to Romey that they were two individuals who would respect one another's autonomy. He realized at this moment that that had been a lie.

There was only one word recognizable in his foggy brain. That word was *mine*.

Without any preamble, Spinelli crashed his lips into hers. The kiss was not quaint, it was awkward and all-consuming. It was exactly what he was, what he felt, and what he needed. His mouth moved over Romey's hungrily. For her part, Romey met each movement of his lips stroke for stroke.

When Spinelli gave her a fraction of an inch to catch her breath, she was breathless. She looked dazed. He knew that he was both of those things. He was out of his mind. Completely irrational and mindless.

And he loved it. He craved more of it. He wanted a lot of it. No amount of Romey would ever be enough for him.

They had carefully constructed how their lives were going to fit together. And in this one act, they ripped all their carefully laid plans to shreds. There was no going back to the sterile vows they'd made. Things were getting messy, and he was reveling in it.

Spinelli had no idea how long their kiss had lasted. He felt the sun shift over him. But he paid it little mind.

He drank and drank from Romey's mouth, knowing he would never get enough of this woman. Which was entirely illogical. But logic could show itself out the door.

He wanted to rip off the plastic gloves on his hands and hers so that he could feel the softness of her skin. He wanted her fingertips directly on his skin without the sterile layer. But it might be too much. So he contented himself with their kiss.

Spinelli pressed his lips against hers, simply to feel the soft flesh that was his. *Mine*, the word sounded in his head again, like a chant. He knew that one person could not own another. But he needed to possess this woman's body, mind, and soul. Just the legal papers weren't enough. He needed to imprint himself over her very being so that every man, woman, and child would know to whom she belonged.

What had he been thinking? That he could spend his life in a platonic relationship with the most desirable woman he'd ever met? He was an idiot.

"Romey?"

"Hmmm?"

"I have a confession to make."

"Hmmm."

The confession was that he'd fallen in love with her. More importantly, he'd known it for some time. He'd known it since the first time he'd seen her. He needed to confess that he'd fallen in love with Romey at first sight.

Her eyes were closed. Her chin tilted up towards him, still in that perfect obtuse angle. Spinelli couldn't resist. He ducked his head and stole a kiss at the slope of her neck. Romey sighed against him, curling her hands behind his head and pulling him closer.

Spinelli lost himself at the edge of the polygon that was his wife's long, elegant neck. He kissed up her jawline. Slowly, enjoying the precipice of her chin. When he returned to her lips, he remembered he'd been about to tell her something very important.

"Romey?"

"Hmmm?" she hummed, pressing her lips against his.

Once again, Spinelli forgot his train of thought as he looked down at the perfect creature in his arms. Romey blinked up at him. Her brows furrowed, making perfect arcs over her widening eyes. Her hold around his neck loosened as she stared at him. The golden flecks at the edges of her eyes sparkled at him. Spinelli felt like he was looking into the heart of a supernova, and the star was bursting from within. It should've alarmed him. But it didn't. Because when he looked into Romey's eyes, he felt he was seeing into her soul.

But just like facial expressions, the light from a soul was still confusing for him to read. Was that love reflected back at him? Or simply desire? He wasn't sure? He had no barometer to test it.

What he did understand was the grin that spread across her face. It meant she was happy with him. His head dipped to Romey's and stole another kiss— for data purposes, of course. He planned to collect a host of samples from this woman over a very long trial period that was likely to last a lifetime.

So engrossed in the kiss were they that they didn't hear the door opening until the sharp intake of air split them apart. Standing in the entryway to the enclosed garden were Jules and Porco. Spinelli's friend winked at him, while his sister-in-law pointed an accusatory finger at Spinelli and Romey.

"I told you so!" Jules beamed as she waggled her finger at the couple.

Spinelli was busted. He had fallen in love, and he didn't care who knew about it. Unfortunately, he'd have to wait to tell his wife. He didn't want to make more of a spectacle with Jules and Porco present.

CHAPTER SIXTEEN

"*R*omey and Jordan sitting in a tree."

Romey ignored the singsong voice trailing behind her. Unlike other eldest siblings, she hadn't had a year or more to herself before Jules had intruded on her only child status. Her twin had been born the same day and had begun annoying her only moments after her appearance.

"K I S S I N G."

"Really, Jules? Are we twelve?"

Romey had more important matters to tend to. Thinking about the kiss she'd just shared with her husband had to wait a few minutes. Even though she was having trouble pushing the memory down. She could still feel the press of his lips against hers. The rough texture of his thumb on her cheek. The buttery taste of him lingered on her tongue.

Had he had toast for breakfast?

The moisture in the air was not helping her think straight. Neither was the rising temperature inside the garden enclosure. Moisture plus heat equaled humidity. There was far too much of it in the space.

At the temperature panel, Romey adjusted the controls for the heat. When she looked at the temperature, she saw it was at normal levels.

Odd. It was nowhere near as hot as she felt. But still, she wanted to peel out of her T-shirt. She needed a towel to sponge herself off. Perhaps it wasn't the atmosphere in the room. Perhaps it was the residual effects of that K I S S I N Ging with her husband.

Her lips still tingled at the thought. Not just the thought, the memory. Romey had had her first kiss just a few minutes ago.

Well, technically, it wasn't her first kiss. But that fumbling, wet slobber she'd let Sundance Lightfoot plant on her by the creek when they were sixteen no longer counted.

Jordan had been masterful with his mouth. And that thing he'd done with his tongue. Oh yes, she wanted to study that some more. For research purposes, of course.

Who was she kidding? She wanted to experience it again just for the pleasure of it.

"First came marriage, then came love. Next comes the baby in the baby carriage."

Romey stiffened at that. She and Jordan had started a conversation about progeny. Now that they were moving closer to activities that involved creating children, they should probably talk about it later tonight.

Later? The thought of nightfall sent her mind to more carnal thoughts. Would their sleeping arrangements change now that they were kissing? Did she want them too?

She felt like her mind was leaking all rational thought. *Drip* there went an IQ point as she wondered if she could replace the expired makeup kit so that she could make herself pretty for dinner. *Drip,* there went a couple hundred SAT points as she racked her brain over what outfit she should wear when Jordan came home tonight.

Looking down, Romey saw that her hand was wet. Was her brain actually leaking out of her head? Or was there an actual leak in her garden's plumbing system? Romey dropped to her knees to investigate.

A single leak in the structure could stymie the entire process.

"For a woman that was getting thoroughly snogged a moment ago, you don't look too happy about it."

From her place on the floor underneath the plant's containers, Romey let out an exasperated sigh. Not at her sister's poking and prodding. She was used to that.

"Snog? Really, Jules? Are you twelfth century now?" Their father was overly fond of Elizabethan terminology. "I'm very happy about the progression of my relationship with the man I've chosen to be my partner for life. But I'm not going to lose my mind over it."

Of course, just then a drop of water landed splat on Romey's forehead

"Yeah, right," Jules smirked, looking down on her twin.

"Our vows are still intact. We are just adding to them."

"Conjugal visits, you mean."

"Jules, don't be crass."

"Romey, don't be a stick in the mud. Admit it, you have feelings for Jordan. Just say it. It'll make you sound normal."

"It's perfectly natural for one to desire one's husband." Jules traced the lining of the pipe until she found the source of the moisture. There was a clog there.

"Hmm, and love him."

Romey opened her mouth to argue, but another drop of water fell right into her mouth. She coughed and spluttered. The mixture that she used to nurture her plants wasn't toxic, but that didn't mean it tasted yummy.

"There was a bet going, you know," said Jules. "To see how long before passion took over and the two of you jumped each other."

Romey focused on the drip. There might be a loose valve or connection. Or there might be a root mass clogging the reservoir.

"I gave it a week. I can't believe I was so far off. Porco won. He gave it a day."

Finally, Romey found the source of the problem. One plant had doubled up and grown beyond the capacity of its container. Its roots had punctured the container. She'd have to rehouse the big guy. But for now, some duck tape would suffice.

"I'm happy you two realized you're in love."

Romey sat up. She didn't meet her sister's gaze. Instead, she reached for a towel to wipe the residual water from her hands. The dripping had stopped, but there was a puddle of water on the floor. Romey had stopped the symptom, but she doubted that she'd found the source. She'd have to search deeper. The system she'd designed was so interconnected that one wrong move could spell disaster.

"Rome, admit it."

"I won't admit that. It makes me feel out of control."

Jules joined her sister on the floor. "You don't have to control it, Rome. Just let it be."

Romey reached over with the towel and wiped up the puddle on the floor. The stone of the ground stayed moist after the water was gone. Only a bit of heat would lift the rest of the moisture from the surface. Romey decided to let the spot remain. It would evaporate soon enough.

CHAPTER SEVENTEEN

"*A*ssault team, move."

"Roger, that."

Spinelli watched on the big screens as the men moved along the corridor. Weapons were raised. Expressions were pensive, watchful as the men were on high alert.

Beside him, Commander South watched the monitors. His steely expression gave away nothing of what he was thinking of the changes Spinelli had instituted. Spinelli wished the man would wince or frown. But his lips stayed in a straight line as did his eyebrows. He could not get a read on the man.

"West, Nile, cover Jasper. Rice and I will flank."

"Copy that, Red Leader."

Gunshots rang out, sounding like the real thing

across the speakers because it was the real thing. Spinelli had recorded the sound and written code to ensure that the sound played with each press one of the players made on the trigger. He'd recorded the sound of a body being impacted as well. Not a real body, but he'd taken pains to ensure the mass he'd used had the same density so that the sound would be realistic. Once a soldier in combat heard that sound, they would never forget it. The game needed to remind them, needed to reinforce to each man and woman the realness of war.

As the team advanced, more problems came there way. But not a multitude of them. Instead of infinite possibilities, Spinelli had used the Golden Ratio of the Fibonacci sequence. The variables increased by the sum of the previous two numbers. So the pressure never let up, but it consistently challenged the player in levels of difficulty.

It didn't look like it was working. On the monitors, the team's heartbeats were up. Their adrenalin was spiked high. They'd conquered the first set of obstacles in their way. But as the hurdles multiplied, the group became taxed. They weren't going to reach their target. Already they were falling back.

The speakers reverberated with the clanging

bang of an explosion. Commander South did wince then. His facial features contorted as though he remembered the pain that being anywhere near a bomb renders to the ears and nose as well as the body. Spinelli had gotten the authentic sound of that, too.

The men were blown back. In the real world, they would not have survived the explosion, so the game caused their life forces to deplete. It was over. The men had lost, and it looked like Spinelli had lost the contract.

He glanced behind him at Rusty, who leaned against the wall. Rusty wore the same pensive expression as the Commander. But Spinelli saw defeat in his friend's gaze. Only because Spinelli knew what that particular expression looked like on Rusty's face. Rusty now wore the same expression he'd had as when he'd gotten his divorce papers.

"Good work."

Spinelli blinked. He looked down at the control panel. He didn't remember recording that voice command. Definitely not in Commander South's deep baritone.

"I'm sorry?" said Spinelli. "Come again, sir?"

"I said, good work, soldier. You listened to my instructions, and you incorporated the changes."

Spinelli could only stare at the commander. When he still couldn't comprehend, he turned to Rusty. But Rusty wore the same confused expression as Spinelli.

"There were only able to make it to the next level of play," said Spinelli. "They didn't win the game, sir."

"Exactly," said Commander South. "They were able to advance with the new changes, but they weren't defeated. Now they have something new to work on."

Spinelli still wasn't getting it. When he played a game, he played it to win.

"You know there are battles won and lost in a war. If we succeeded against every obstacle put in our way, we would never learn from our mistakes. This version of the game pushed them. It challenged them to go to the extremes without defeating them. Excellent work."

Commander South held out his hand. Spinelli eyed the outstretched hand with wonder. He'd done it. He'd won the contract. This would be a boon to the camp. Now they could boast a state of the art physical course as well as virtual war games.

"I'm glad you liked the changes," said Spinelli,

clasping the commander's hand. "They were inspired by my wife, actually."

"You're married?"

"Yes," said Spinelli. "Only a few days now."

They had been the best days of his life. Today being ranked number one after that kiss he'd shared with Romey. If Jules and Porco hadn't barged in on them, and if he didn't have this appointment to make, he'd still have his wife in his arms. In fact, he had nothing left to do here today, and he wanted to celebrate this victory. There was only one person who he wanted to share his accomplishment with.

"This team got here a few months ago," said the Commander. "And now you're all married?

That was true. The six of them had come to the ranch as single men. Before setting foot on the Purple Heart Ranch's soil, they'd all scoffed at the idea of marriage. Yet here they all were, happily hitched.

All but Rusty. His marriage was over. Despite the lore surrounding this ranch, Spinelli doubted the man would ever marry again.

"I want to show Tactical Approach to the FSW group."

Spinelli opened his mouth, but no words came out. The FSW group? That was the makers of Full

Spectrum War, the game that had inspired Spinelli to join the Army.

"I think those fellas would have a lot of use for a mind like yours."

Again, Spinelli opened his mouth, but words escaped him. That had been a dream of his, to work with FSW. The offers hadn't been forthcoming after he was discharged from the Army Rangers. So, he'd gone into business with his friends. But now?

"Walk with me," said the Commander. "I see great things in your future."

Spinelli followed after the commander on wobbly legs. Every dream he ever had and dared not to have was coming true all in the space of one day. It was as though the Golden Ratio had come to life in his world.

CHAPTER EIGHTEEN

"Ouch!"

Romey dropped the knife and brought her thumb to her mouth. The small nick of blood tasted metallic on her tongue mixed with the savory hint of spring onion. Together, the open wound and the ripe onion stung, and she yanked her finger from her mouth.

By the time she pulled her injured finger from her mouth, the blood had dried up. No need for a bandage. She moved to the kitchen sink to shove her finger under a cool spray of faucet water instead.

The first droplet hit her flesh, soothing the wound. From the corner of her eye, she saw red. The flames on the stove rose high. The water from the pot boiled over on the stove.

Leaving the faucet running, Romey dashed into action to save the noodles inside the pot. But it was too late. The contents of the pot spilled over, dousing the fire and spilling all over the stovetop.

"Don't forget the pan of beans," Jules said around a mouthful of popcorn.

On a back burner, the pan of beans was having the opposite problem. All of its water had evaporated. The small green pods were now brown and black as they clung to the bottom of the pan.

"They never stood a chance." Jules adjusted the bowl in her lap. Her feet were propped on another chair as she leaned back, watching her sister's every failing move.

"You could help, you know," growled Romey as she turned all the burners on the stove off.

"And miss the evening's entertainment? Heck, no." Her sister chomped on more popcorn from the bowl in her lap. The grin on her face and sparkle in her eyes told Romey that Jules was, in fact, enjoying the sideshow of this foodie fiasco. "I never thought I'd see the day when you were domesticated."

Romey ignored the words she knew her sister meant as a jab. Looking down at the mess she'd made, Romey huffed as she realized not a single dish was edible. Cooking was not her strong suit.

When she got hungry, she'd simply tug something out of the ground, or out of one of her hydroponic containers, and pop it into her mouth. Raw eating was not just a way of life for her, it was pretty much all she knew how to do. Introducing heat to food was unnecessary. Except now that she had a husband whose lovely muscles could not subsist on raw plants alone.

Of course, Romey knew that a plant-based diet could sustain a man of Jordan's bulk. There had been plenty of studies of vegan athletes. But all of those men and women had lean muscle. Romey liked Jordan's size and shape just the way he was.

To keep him just the way he was, she'd have to learn to take care of him. More than one study showed that a way to a man's heart was through his stomach. So, here she was. Trying to learn how to cook starchy proteins. She wasn't ready to tackle meat.

Romey wasn't an animal activist. She was a complete Darwinist and believed it was a survival of the fittest, dog-eat-dog, kinda world. But if she couldn't cook a bean or a grain yet, to put a piece of red meat in her hands would definitely be animal cruelty.

"Honey, we're home." David's loud voice boomed

from the front door, carrying it easily to the kitchen at the back of the house.

"In here," Jules mumble-shouted through another handful of popcorn.

David came in and scooped his wife up out of the chair and into his arms. He planted a long kiss on her lips. "Mmm. Buttery."

Romey wasn't one for butter or oils. There was no need when most of her diet consisted of raw foods. But if fire and condiments are what it took to get her husband to sweep her off her feet like that, Romey was ready to go find a cow.

She heard movement in the other room. The sound of a bag being dropped in the doorway. The *thunk* of thick-soled boots sounded on the hardwoods; Jordan.

He appeared in the entryway of the kitchen. His eyes glanced at Jules and David, still wrapped up in their embrace. He frowned at the two lovebirds.

Was that a look of disapproval? Did Jordan not believe in public displays of affection? Did she? Perhaps if she could get him alone, he might show her the affection he did earlier today in her garden.

Or perhaps that had been a one-time event? They'd agreed to introduce a physical aspect to their marriage. But they hadn't discussed the particulars.

Finally, Jordan's gaze lifted to find her. The frown on his face eased. His brows lowered as he took her in.

Romey stayed rooted while Jordan made his way around the entwined couple to stand before her. He offered her a bright smile. Then he bent down and kissed her cheek.

It was just a simple brush of his lips on her flesh. The contact made her entire face heat. She felt a *thud* as her heart skipped a beat, and then raced to catch up. The muscles in her belly twisted in hunger.

"Hi," he said.

"Hi," she mimicked.

"You're cooking?" Jordan's brows raised, no doubt taking in the catastrophe of her efforts. "I thought you said you weren't good at that."

"I'm not. I'm trying to learn, to improve myself."

His smile went brighter, so bright that Romey felt the urge to shield her eyes from the brilliance of it. She didn't dare. She didn't want to miss a single ray of her husband's shine.

"You're practicing the Michelangelo Phenomenon?"

Romey nodded. Though it wasn't following the letter of the phenomenon. She wanted to better herself, but not necessarily for their mutual partnership. Romey was making these changes because she wanted Jordan to value her more. She wanted him to see her as more than a partner. She wanted him to see her as a lover.

Though by the burned beans and overcooked noodles, she didn't see her chances looking good.

"It's a trial and error thing," she said. "The first iteration didn't go as planned. But I've analyzed what went wrong. I believe in the second trial, I can improve on my mistakes and have a fairly successful outcome."

Jordan looked past her at the disaster on the stove. Jules and David had unlocked their lips and were doing the same. From the screen door, Hamlet looked inside, took a whiff, and promptly turned tail and trotted away.

Great. She'd completely failed. She was not going to win her husband's heart through his stomach.

"It's fine, Rome," Jordan grinned. "We brought dinner from Patel's. All vegan."

Pastor Patel's family restaurant was one of the few the folks from the commune ate at in the town. Many of the Indian dishes were vegetable dishes. Those that had milk or cream could easily be made without and still tasted delectable.

"Have a seat, ladies," said David, pulling out a chair for his wife. "We're celebrating."

"We are?" asked Jules. "What amazing thing did you accomplish today, my darling husband?"

"Not me. Spinelli."

Romey sat down in the chair offered to her by her husband. He scooted her into the table and then took a moment to unbag the take out they'd brought home. Once the women were served, he took his seat. But no one picked up a fork to dig in.

"Aren't you going to tell her your good news, Spinelli?" said David.

Jordan took in a deep breath. His massive shoulders rising and falling with the movement. "The war game module I've been working on had its final review today..."

"And?" Romey prompted after Jordan took one too many seconds to continue.

He glanced over at her and grinned. The sheer joy and childlike amusement in the expression made her shiver with pleasure. The grin was only for her. She realized he wanted her to be proud of whatever he'd accomplished today. At this moment, she understood why it was called the Michelangelo Phenomenon because her husband looked like a

masterpiece as he shared his proud moment
with her.

"And they loved it," he said.

"Of course they loved it," said Romey. "You're
brilliant."

"No, I screwed up on the first try. But I was able
to win them over. That was all because of you."

"Me?"

"I reprogrammed the game with the Golden
Ratio from the Fibonacci Sequence." His gaze
slipped to the spirals dangling from her ears. "You
inspired me."

"That's amazing." Romey found herself rising
and flinging herself into Jordan's arms. He caught
her and squeezed her. It was too late to feel
embarrassed, and she didn't. All she felt was her
husband's warmth surrounding her.

"Hey, Jules," said David. "How about a picnic
dinner down by the creek?"

"But—"

David grabbed his wife's hand and a couple of
containers. He ushered them to the door. Jules,
annoying little sister that she was, made kissing
noises as they went out the door. A hopeful Hamlet
was hot on their trail.

"I am so proud of you," Romey said. She was

sitting on Jordan's lap. He hadn't asked her to move. Instead, his arms wrapped tighter around her middle.

"I didn't tell you the best part yet. The Commander was so impressed by Tactical Approach that he wants me to consult with FSW."

Romey had a vague idea of who FSW was. Jordan had talked about his admiration for the group. She supposed she should've been paying closer attention when he spoke about his career and the players. But she had all the time in the world to ask him more about it another time. Right now, Romey was angling how to show her husband just how much she appreciated him with a kiss. But she had never initiated a kiss before.

"It would be a six-month consulting job," Jordan was saying. "They're headquartered in DC"

Romey had been glancing at her husband's mouth, trying to decide how to make her approach. But those two letters threw cold water on her face.

"DC?"

Jordan's gaze had fallen to her mouth. He moved closer, preparing to make an approach of his own. But Romey jerked away.

"You're moving to DC?"

CHAPTER NINETEEN

How had he gotten so lucky? The woman on his lap was the smartest woman he'd ever met. Most men were dazzled by makeup or revealing clothing. His Romey had inspired him with the earrings dangling from her perfectly plump earlobes.

Romey was the most beautiful woman Spinelli had ever seen. There was a light that shone from her eyes that always made it easier to tell what she was thinking. Her heart-shaped mouth would stretch up in a smile when she was pleased. Or it would tug down into a frown when she was thinking. Making it so easy for him to comprehend.

Spinelli loved those expressions the best because he'd wait in anticipation of what she would say.

Right now, her gaze was narrowed on him. So much so that a pinprick of light couldn't escape the squint of her eyes.

What could that mean? She had a new idea but was thinking something over?

He thought a new problem was unlikely. Her mouth was drawn in a thin line, neither pleased nor considering. Spinelli wasn't sure what she was thinking, but he got the sense that it wasn't good.

His wife shouldn't be thinking at all in his arms, that's not how seduction went. He might not have a lot of experience with women, but desire he knew. Mainly because he felt it like he had for no other with this woman in his arms. So why was she pushing him away?

"You're moving to Washington, DC?"

Romey climbed off his lap. She didn't retake the seat beside him. She paced a small line in front of him, back and forth with her arms crossed over her chest.

Spinelli might not be good at expressions, but actions he was much better at reading. That pacing and the arms closing her off to him in a protective gesture all read agitation. But what could she be upset about? Maybe he hadn't made things clear, and she needed more details.

"Yes," he confirmed. "For six months. If I get the contract. But it's as good as done. The Commander has many friends high up. I've always hated that aspect of business dealings. Promotion should rely on what you know, not who you know. Would you agree?"

The pacing came to a halt. Romey's head snapped around. She glared down at him. That expressive light he loved so much in her eyes looked like hot, red flames. That was definitely anger in her eyes. But why?

"I'm gathering that you're not happy about this?" Spinelli hedged.

"You think?"

That was the definition of a rhetorical question. She'd asked the question but definitely didn't expect an answer. So, he asked a question of his own. "What have I done to deserve your ire?"

"You're taking a job all the way across the country for six months. You didn't consult me. And you think I'm supposed to be happy about all of this."

Those were all valid points. Points he probably should've considered in hindsight. "I can see where I might've made a misstep in this process."

"Might've?"

"I assumed you'd be pleased as this opportunity would elevate my status in my career, thus elevating our partnership."

"Our partnership?" Her voice had gone up a few octaves. "We're married."

"I know we're married. I was there when we wrote our vows."

"Oh, now you're throwing that vow of autonomy in my face?"

"No, I'm not. That would be keeping score."

Romey's eyes blazed even brighter. She uncrossed her arms from her chest. Her fists balled at her sides. Another motion that Spinelli knew was one of aggression.

He held up his hands. "Not that I'm accusing you of keeping score."

"Well, I am. I'm breaking the Communal Orientation vow right here, right now. You made a unilateral decision that affects our union without consulting me. I am having an emotional response to it."

"That's two. So? We're even?"

If it was possible, Romey's gaze widened further. Her mouth gaped open. Once more, Spinelli had said the wrong thing. He was entirely out of his depths here. He didn't dare bring up another of their vows. He had the suspicion that a logical argument would not work in his favor with his wife so emotional at the moment.

All he wanted to do was share his joy with this woman. Take her into his arms. Tell her he was in love with her. Then kiss her senseless for the rest of the night. It was irrational, but he couldn't think of another thing to do.

He reached for her. She turned her head away from him, but she didn't fight his hold.

"This was supposed to be the happiest day of my life," Spinelli began. "I have the woman of my dreams, and I was offered my dream job."

Romey inhaled. A shudder went through her shoulders as she did so. When she turned to him, there were tears in her eyes.

Spinelli was horrified to see the tears there. Finally, he was reading someone's expressions perfectly clearly. Yet even though he could read her expression, he had no idea what to do about it.

He wouldn't have the opportunity to do anything about it. Romey stormed past him and into her bedroom, slamming the door shut behind her.

CHAPTER TWENTY

*R*omey couldn't remember the last time she was this angry. Perhaps when the NASA Terrestrial Planet Finder space missions had been canceled. Or Pluto had been demoted from planet status. Or Douglas Prasher had been denied the Nobel Peace Prize in chemistry for his work on the green fluorescent protein. Oh, that had boiled Romey's onions something good.

But none of those moments could top the feeling of her husband choosing a job over her.

Romey had gone to bed angry, slamming her bedroom door in Jordan's face for effect. The idiot hadn't tried knocking on her door or calling out to her. She'd heard him sigh, and then the thunking tread of his boots on the hardwood floor as he retreated to his own room.

He'd gone back to his own room when she'd planned for them to stay in the same room from this night forward. But no, he was going to have a room in Washington, DC. All to play video games for six months.

Jordan's logical argument played over and over in Romey's mind. He's said it was his dream job. She didn't doubt that it would raise his profile in the virtual war games industry, thus being a boon for their future. She had heard him when he'd said it was temporary.

It was a smart decision. If he'd made it before yesterday when they had taken their relationship to a new level, back then, she might be willing to accept it. But not today.

Today she was an emotional mess.

Jordan hadn't broken any promises to her. Everything he'd decided on was entirely within the bounds of the vows they'd made to one another. Romey wanted to rip up those rational rites.

She didn't want her husband to see her as a positive illusion. She wanted her husband to be delusional in his love for her. She wanted to call Michelangelo and his drivel of supporting a partner's growth a farce. She didn't want her own autonomy. She wanted her life inextricably intertwined with her husband's so that he wouldn't go away, and he would stay with her.

When Romey woke in the morning, heart in hand, prepared to renegotiate her vows with Jordan, she found his room empty.

Her back sagged against the doorframe. Her heart didn't skip a beat at his absence. It slowed as though trying to comprehend the emptiness spreading throughout its chambers.

Romey knew her heart wasn't empty. There was oxygen-rich blood pumping into and out of her valves and headed to her lungs. So why was she having trouble breathing?

It made no logical sense, except that it was nonsense. Because she was in love. She might as well admit to all the foolishness of it. She had nothing left to lose. But she wasn't going to be one of those women that chased after the man. No, if Jordan wanted to talk, he'd have to come and find her.

She supposed he didn't want to talk. Being that he hadn't come after her last night. And he'd gotten up before the crack of dawn this morning to avoid her.

Romey shut her husband's bedroom door and

made her way out of the house. The sun was peaking over the horizon as she made her way to her greenhouse. Plenty of the commune's residents were already up, hard at work on the crops that were their livelihood.

In a few hours, Romey would be escorting her science class to the county science fair. But first, she had to tend to her garden. If she could focus, she might determine what the problem was in her hydroponic garden before the whole system broke down.

Opening the door to the greenhouse, Romey heard the sounds of movement. Laying on the floor beneath her containers were a pair of jean-clad legs. Her heartbeat roared back to life, playing a fast rhythm. Whose song died a second later.

The jean-clad legs ended in a pair of Birkenstocks. Her sensible Jordan wouldn't be caught dead in the footwear. Paris slid out from under the containers with a grin on his face.

"Hey," he said. "I came in to find you and saw that your pump was malfunctioning."

Romey looked down at the water pump. Its function was to push the nutrient solution to all of the plants in the system. How had she not considered that it might be the problem from yesterday?

Whatever had happened, it wasn't a problem any longer. The nutrients flowed freely. The plants were already lifting their heads. The system was back online.

"Thank you, Paris. You didn't have to do this."

"What? You think I'd just turn my back and walk away if I saw you were in a bind?" He scoffed, wiping his hands on his pants. "What kind of man would that make me?"

What kind of man, indeed.

Romey looked Paris over. His leaned build was courtesy of all the hours he spent tending to plants in the fields, not hefting guns or taking down bad guys. He had a gentle spirit. He also had a number of academic degrees to match her own.

"Look, Rome, I'm sorry about the other day; what I said about not getting the inspectors in here to certify your hydroponics. This place is as much part of the farm as anything. When they arrive next week, we'll bring them in here."

Tears stung her eyes. Romey wasn't prone to emotional outbursts, but everything inside her was in chaos today. Was his outpouring evidence that she had feelings for Paris?

Maybe she should've married him instead? She and Paris had similar interests. They were both tied to this land and wouldn't leave to spend six months in the nation's capital playing video games. And she was sure that she wouldn't be prone to nonsensical emotions with Paris.

Paris Montgomery was a gentle, passive soul. Except for that time when he'd punched David in the eye over Jules. Twice.

No man had ever punched anyone for Romey. Not that she wanted that. What she wanted was for someone to be passionate enough about her to do it.

"Romey? What is it? What's wrong?"

She blinked her eyelids rapidly. But just like windshield wipers fighting a downpour, she was still having trouble bringing Paris into focus under the deluge of tears.

"Is it your husband? Am I going to have to have words with him? Or maybe use my fists instead of my words?"

"You'd do that for me?" Romey hiccupped. "You'd punch a man for me?"

"Of course, I would if you needed defending."

What a beautiful, passionate statement. So, why didn't that get her heart racing? Paris hugged her tightly in his arms. She didn't feel engulfed as she had when Jordan held her. She didn't have the sense of falling while at the same time knowing she was secure.

"I don't want you to punch Jordan in the nose. I want to kick him in the shins."

Paris pulled back and looked down at her. "Sounds like you're in love with him."

"I am," she sighed.

"You don't sound happy about it."

"Love is awful. It's entirely illogical and unpredictable. It's messy, and sometimes it hurts. The worst part is that I don't think he feels the same way."

"Why would you think that?"

"He's planning to leave me. Well, not leave me—leave me." Wow, she'd just used a phrase to describe itself. "He's going on a long trip without me. I don't want to be apart from him for that long. Just the thought of it makes my heart feel like it's breaking. If he doesn't feel the same way…"

Romey put her hands over her eyes. She tried to wipe away the tears there, but more fell to take their place.

"I've seen the way he looks at you," said Paris. "It's the same way that Porco looks at Jules, like she's the reason he breathes. I've never looked at anyone that way... unless it was a plant."

But Romey knew that Jordan was out in the world, breathing just fine while she was out of his sight. She wanted to believe he loved her, but she wasn't so sure. What she did know is that she would have trouble breathing without him in her life.

Already her heart was throbbing, her lungs felt constricted, her head was a mess. She felt out of control, like an unbalanced equation with too many variables. She had no idea how to solve this problem.

CHAPTER TWENTY-ONE

Spinelli pounded at his chest, but it still ached from the inside out. All night and into the day, he couldn't shake the sensation that his lungs weren't inflated properly. Despite taking deep breaths, he felt like he couldn't breathe.

After Romey had slammed her bedroom door in his face, Spinelli had stared at the door frame in shock, uncertain what to do. He'd wanted to knock the door down, burst inside... and say what?

He hadn't a clue what to say to her? He'd offered up a reasoned argument and was met with an irrational, emotional female. Completely unlike the levelheaded, even-tempered, thoughtful woman he'd married.

"You look awful," Rusty said as he came into the control room.

The space was empty this early in the morning. They weren't due to have another training session until later in the day. Spinelli had already uploaded the program and reorganized the arena. Now he sat slumped in his chair.

"I feel awful," he said.

His eyes felt as though there was sand in the corners. Every beat of his heart irritated his chest. His fingers alternated from numb to achy every other minute. His neck muscles ached from trying to hold his head up when all he wanted to do was lie down. Instead, Spinelli let his head loll back against the chair's headrest. That's when he got a look at his friend.

There were dark bags under Rusty's eyes. The man's skin was so pale, it looked like he hadn't seen the sun in days. There was a sickly look around his mouth, as though he could puke at any moment.

"Speaking of awful," said Spinelli, "have you looked in the mirror yourself today?"

Rusty grabbed the seat beside Spinelli. Instead of holding his head high, he let his forehead fall into his palm. A long, weary sigh escaped his lips. "I signed the papers this morning."

Spinelli didn't need to ask which papers Rusty was referring to. It was no wonder the man looked a wreck. His marriage had officially ended.

"I thought you were going to fight for her?" said Spinelli.

"I did everything I could." Rusty opened both of his palms, but there was nothing in his hands. " I reasoned. I pleaded. I even cried. But when a woman's fed up, there's nothing you can do about it."

"Why was she fed up?"

"She said I was never there for her."

"Because you had to work?"

Rusty pursed his lips, shaking his head sadly. "I don't think she meant physically."

What other ways were there to be present for someone other than physically? Spinelli looked over at the glass window of the arena's enclosure. With the lights off, the glass was reflective. Spinelli saw that he and Rusty looked like twins. Did that mean that his marriage was over? That was the last thing he wanted.

"Romey and I had a fight."

"Whatever you did, you were wrong. Tell her you're sorry."

"I don't know what I did wrong?" Now it was Spinelli that held up empty palms. "I told her we won the virtual war game contract. Then I told her about the offer to work for FSW in DC. I outlined the benefits that taking the job would have to our union, and she blew up at me."

Once again, Spinelli leaned his head back against the chair. The pressure was so heavy on the crown of his head that he allowed his eyes to close. In his mind's eye, all he saw was Romey. His inner world felt full with Romey in it. Now that she was out of his reach, he felt empty.

"Oh, you idiot."

Spinelli blinked his eyes open. His head snapped upright until he was eye level with Rusty. His expression was one that was easy to read; curled lip, wrinkled nose, unblinking gaze. The man wore a disgusted look on his face.

"How am I the idiot in this?" Spinelli spluttered.

"Would you really do it? Would you leave your wife?"

The very thought left Spinelli feeling feverish. The weight increased on his forehead and shoulders by the ton. His hands balled into fists with the need to punch through something.

"Never," he said. "It's just for a few months."

"You could do that? You could be away from her for that long?"

Spinelli opened his mouth, but the words stuck in his throat. He thought he'd thought this through. Truthfully, it hadn't occurred to him that Romey wouldn't be with him as he caught hold of this particular dream. He'd imagined her by his side for every moment of it. Didn't she know that?

What if she didn't know that? What if she wouldn't do that?

"I barely made it a night without her," he said. "I love her so much that everything looks gray when she's not there."

He knew that waxed philosophic, but it was true. The green of the commune hadn't looked at all vibrant this morning when he'd stepped outside. He'd done most of his work today in a dimly lit room while looking at a black and white screen. Even his wardrobe was a gray shirt and drab fatigues.

"Does she know how you feel about her?" asked Rusty. "Have you actually told her that you're in love with her?"

Spinelli shook his head. He'd been about to the other day after that kiss. But then they'd been interrupted. And later that evening, before he could admit to his feelings, she'd slammed a door in his face.

If she thought he'd so callously leave her behind,

would she even believe that he had real feelings for her? Would a woman as rational and logical as Romey even accept such a notion as fact?

"I can't just tell her this," said Spinelli. "I need to prove it."

"Prove what?"

"That I love her."

Regardless of what she might think of him, Spinelli needed her to know this one thing. He knew just how to present the findings to her. But first, he had to find her.

CHAPTER TWENTY-TWO

*R*omey stood from her crouch. The tendons in her knees and spine all crackled with protest as she did so. She'd just helped her last student put up their experiment for the science fair. The actual work of lugging the projects inside the church recreation room hadn't been taxing. Keeping the fake smile plastered on her face while her heart was in agony had been.

She wished she could put the temperamental organ in a jar of vinegar and have it congeal like one of those bouncy eggs. Right now, her heart felt like a volcanic mixture just waiting for a teaspoon of baking soda to make it erupt and spill all over the church's linoleum floors.

Love sucked. But she was in it. And she didn't see an escape.

Jordan had stolen into her mind and lodged himself in both her left and right brain. She was emotionally attached to him. She couldn't reason her way out of it.

"We have a late addition to this year's fair," called Pastor Vance from a podium at the front of the room.

It wasn't lost on Romey that the town's church held the annual event. None of the holy men who'd graced these hallowed halls had ever looked at science as a nefarious practice. They encouraged anything that would open the hearts and expand the minds of their flock, especially the young. Romey might not attend church here every Sunday, but she'd always felt at home within these walls.

"As you know," Pastor Vance continued, "the fair is open to young and old. I believe this may be our oldest participant."

The youth participants all left their table to get a look at the old-timer who was their new competition. Behind the children, parents flocked to see the show. Her curiosity getting the better of her, Romey made her way to the edges of the crowd and then gasped at what she saw.

Jordan stood at the front of the crowd. He was

dressed in his usual T-shirt, fatigues, and heavy boots. He was surrounded by posters of data readouts and printed charts of colored graphs. He had a pencil shoved behind his ear as he addressed the crowd. It took Romey a moment to tune into his words. Just the sight of him leading a lecture was the sexiest thing she'd ever seen in her life.

"It has been asked many times if love can be quantified," he began. "It's a difficult question as not many agree on what love actually is. Some say it's a physical force. Then there are those who say it is an ethereal experience of the soul. The only consensus is that it can be felt. Well, feelings are electrical."

Jordan turned his back and walked over to his friend Anthony Keaton. Keaton sat in a chair with LEDs attached to his forehead. A square monitor faced the crowd. On the screen, lines ran at steady crests and valleys.

"I'm measuring the levels of dopamine and serotonin present in his brain." Jordan made a motion to a woman to step forward.

When Brenda Vance stepped in her husband's line of sight, the crests went mountain high, barely coming back down into the valleys.

"Notice how the levels increase when the object of love is presented in front of the subject."

Keaton reached for Brenda's hand. When she gave it to him, the lines jumped to the top of the screen. A murmur rose in the crowd as everyone eyed the spikes on the monitor.

Jordan turned from that love-struck couple to another. Dylan Banks from the Purple Heart Ranch stood nearby. He wore a pair of cargo shorts that put his prosthetic leg on display. No one was looking down. All eyes were focused on the wires running under his shirt.

"I've heard it said that when someone falls in love, they feel butterflies in their stomach," Jordan said.

Both Jules and David had made that absurd statement, which both Romey and Jordan had scoffed at. Then Romey had felt the pleasant buzz of insects overtaking her abdomen and learned the error of her beliefs. Though Romey had experiential proof, she watched her husband with rapt attention, eager to see how he'd use science to prove that her feelings were real.

"No butterfly, nor any other insect, could survive in the hydrochloric acid of the stomach."

Romey's stomach clenched at the dismissal. She wanted to shout at Jordan that he was wrong. That she'd felt it.

"What you're actually experiencing is a function of the nervous system. When you see the object of your desire, your body goes into an alert mode similar to the fight or flight mode. Your nervous system releases adrenaline, which shunts the blood away from the gut, causing the muscles there to slow and relax."

Maggie Banks stepped around a corner. When Dylan spied his wife, his eyes lit up, and a secretive smile spread across his handsome face. On the monitor, the readout lines, which had been on a steady plateau up until this point, slumped downward like a butterfly flapping its wings to land on an open flower petal.

Romey wanted to applaud. She wanted to cheer. She wanted to be a part of this experiment so that she might coauthor an academic paper with Jordan on this subject. She could be another of his test subjects because the chemicals in her brain were going haywire. Her stomach muscles were quivering with need. But Jordan wasn't done. And she noted, all through this process, he hadn't once glanced her way.

"They also say that love affects your actions. This is my friend Porco. He loves bacon. But his wife loves tofu."

David sat at a table. A plate rested before him with a few squares that Romey knew to be fried tofu. David wrinkled his nose at the plate of curdled beans. Yet, when he saw Jules, he dug into the dish with zeal.

"You'll see that Porco isn't hooked up to any readouts," said Jordan. "He's simply making a choice to do something he's not interested in for the one he loves."

Jules leaned over and pressed a kiss to her husband's lips as he swallowed. David dropped his fork and embraced his wife. Jules giggled as he nibbled at her lip.

"So you see, love is a mathematical, logical, rational, scientific fact. I know it to be true because I have experienced it firsthand."

Romey looked up to see that her husband's gaze had found her in the crowd. As Jordan walked over to her, in his hand, he held out a document between them.

"These are my test results when I think of my wife."

Romey unrolled the papers. She couldn't read the results. Her eyes were too full of tears. But she didn't need to see the spikes and plateaus to indicate what her husband thought of her. She knew it in her heart. She didn't need any facts to know what he was feeling. He only needed to gaze into her eyes, and she saw it clearly. But he was Jordan, and so he laid out his findings.

"Romey, I have a confession to make; I believe in love at first sight," Jordan said. "From that first moment I saw you in the grocery store, I knew you had to be mine. It started with the intelligence I saw in your eyes. I felt like you understood me, and that made me want to know you. The more I knew, the more I wanted you."

Jordan lifted a hand to her face to catch her tears. More fell as he wiped them away. Looking into his eyes would've overwhelmed Romey if she wasn't so starved for his affection.

"If there is such a thing as love at first sight," she said, "then maybe there is such a thing as love at first sound. I heard you and David talking in the store. David said Jules made his heart speed up and put butterflies in his stomach. You said that wasn't love, it was a medical condition. That's when I fell for you."

Jordan lifted her chin until her lips met his. It was a light kiss, but its impact was big enough to calm the raging sea inside of her. All went quiet, like a lake after a storm. The still waters of her soul ran deeply for this man.

His gaze raked over her face, taking in every detail, and then returning to gaze a little longer. His expression turned serious. "I'll give up D.C. for you."

"Jordan, no."

He shrugged. "It's not tofu."

"It's your dream."

He shook his head slowly. "You are my dream."

Tears stung her eyes. Her husband may not have punched another man for her, but he was willing to turn his back on his passion to please her. This subject was not closed. It would be open to negotiations.

Maybe he could work remotely? Maybe they could lessen the time frame? Maybe she could go with him for part of it?

She'd vowed to this man that she would support his goals, and she would. They'd figure it out. They were two of the smartest people she knew.

"So, we're in love with each other?" she asked.

"I think all the facts point that way. But we could do with a bit more experimenting, just to be sure."

"What procedures did you have in mind?"

A mischievous grin slid over her husband's face.

"I think the next part of our study should be done in a more private laboratory."

"How about my bedroom?"

"Sounds like the perfect setting for this next phase of our experiment."

*R*usty watched as Spinelli and Romey escaped out the doorway. Their absence was noted, but no one said anything. Everyone was far more interested in Spinelli's love experiments. Couples hooked each other up to the devices to get actual proof of what they felt for one another.

It had never occurred to Rusty to question his feelings for Ronnie. It simply was. It was something he'd known about himself to be true. Just as he knew he was a soldier. Just as he knew he could disassemble and reassemble any firearm put in front of him. Just as he knew the right words to say to defuse any crisis situation.

Rusty had talked suicide bombers out of their vests. He'd talked gun-totting assailants into laying down their arms. He'd talked a few men and women down off ledges. He was very good at getting people to see reason and do what he wanted them to. Except when it came to Ronnie.

The woman had a mind of her own and a will of iron. Two of the things he loved most about her. When she got a notion in her head, it was hard to talk her out of it. Even for the trained crisis negotiator.

For months, Rusty had pleaded with her to reconsider her decision to end their marriage. She hadn't budged. In the end, she'd stopped taking his calls and answering his emails. Rusty hadn't spoken or heard from his wife in weeks.

The strain had taken its toll. It was clear she wasn't going to change her mind. She wasn't going to come back to him. There was nothing left in his bag of tricks. Nothing in his training taught him to talk a woman into staying married when she no longer wanted to be.

So, he'd picked up a pen and finally given her what she wanted. Watching the ink flow from the pen onto the divorce papers had been like signing over his soul. As he watched the ink dry, a cloud had shrouded his shoulders. He felt like he'd just returned from combat, and now he was missing a limb.

No prosthetic could replace what Rusty had lost. He'd spend the rest of his life a widower, knowing that the vibrant woman who was his wife was living a full life without him.

Looking around the room, his eyes were assaulted with the oppressive sights of love. Couples laughing. Couples kissing. Couples play fighting. It was too much for him to bear witness to. So, he slipped out a side door.

The sun was starting to set on this day. Not that it mattered. Day bled into night, which bled into weeks and then months for him. This was how he was going to spend the rest of his life; a shell of his former self.

Suddenly, anger boiled inside of Rusty. He wasn't even thirty years old yet. He still had a full life to live. He owed it to all the people whose lives he'd saved to live it.

His phone buzzed in his pocket. Still holding onto his resolve, Rusty took the device out. At the sight of the name on the caller ID, his heart hammered in his chest, his breath left him, buzzing bees raged in his belly.

"Veronica?"

"Russell? I need you."

Find out if Rusty can win back the only woman for him in
"The Rancher takes his Last Chance at Love!"

Shanae Johnson was raised by Saturday Morning cartoons and After School Specials. She still doesn't understand why there isn't a life lesson that ties the issues of the day together just before bedtime. While she's still waiting for the meaning of it all, she writes stories to try and figure it all out. Her books are wholesome and sweet, but her are heroes are hot and heroines are full of sass!

And by the way, the E elongates the A. So it's pronounced Shan-aaaaaaaa. Perfect for a hero to call out across the moors, or up to a balcony, or to blare outside her window on a boombox. If you hear him calling her name, please send him her way!

You can sign up for Shanae's Reader Group at http://bit.ly/ShanaeJohnsonReaders

Also By Shanae Johnson

The Rangers of Purple Heart

The Rancher takes his Convenient Bride

The Rancher takes his Best Friend's Sister

The Rancher takes his Runaway Bride

The Rancher takes his Star Crossed Love

The Rancher takes his Love at First Sight

The Rancher takes his Last Chance at Love

The Brides of Purple Heart

On His Bended Knee

Hand Over His Heart

Offering His Arm

His Permanent Scar

Having His Back

In Over His Head

Always On His Mind

Every Step He Takes

In His Good Hands

Light Up His Life

Strength to Stand

The Rebel Royals series

The King and the Kindergarten Teacher

The Prince and the Pie Maker

The Duke and the DJ

The Marquis and the Magician's Assistant

The Princess and the Principal